The Daughter's Duty

The Emperor's Conspiracy Prequel

Claire Leggett

BANTILLY
PUBLISHING

First published in the Fantasy Realms: Warlords, Witches and
Wolves anthology in 2020
This edition published by Bantilly Publishing in 2021

The Daughter's Duty: The Emperor's Conspiracy

Mobi format: 978-1-925696-79-0
Print: 978-1-925696-78-3

Cover design by Lana Pecherczyk
Edited by Ann Harth
Copyedited by Teena Raffa-Mulligan
Map by Shona Husk

About the Author

Claire Leggett has loved dragons, magic and everything fantastical since she read The Enchanted Wood by Enid Blyton. As a child she used to sneak to the bottom of the garden in the hope of finding fairies. Alas she never found any, so she brought them alive in her own imagination. Her stories are full of magic, adventure and escape.

When Claire's not writing she can be found creating her own handmade journals, swinging on a sidecar, or in the garden attempting to grow something other than weeds.

Claire lives in Western Australia with her husband, who loves even her most annoying quirks, and is currently learning how to crochet.

You can find her complete book list on her website www.claireleggett.com/books. You can connect with Claire by joining her reader group (http://www.claireleggett.com/reader-group/).

Also by Claire Leggett

Fantasy
<u>The Emperor's Conspiracy</u>
The Daughter's Duty
The Assassin's Gift
The Healer's Curse
The Servant's Grace

Claire also writes contemporary romance and romantic suspense under the pen name Claire Boston.
www.claireboston.com

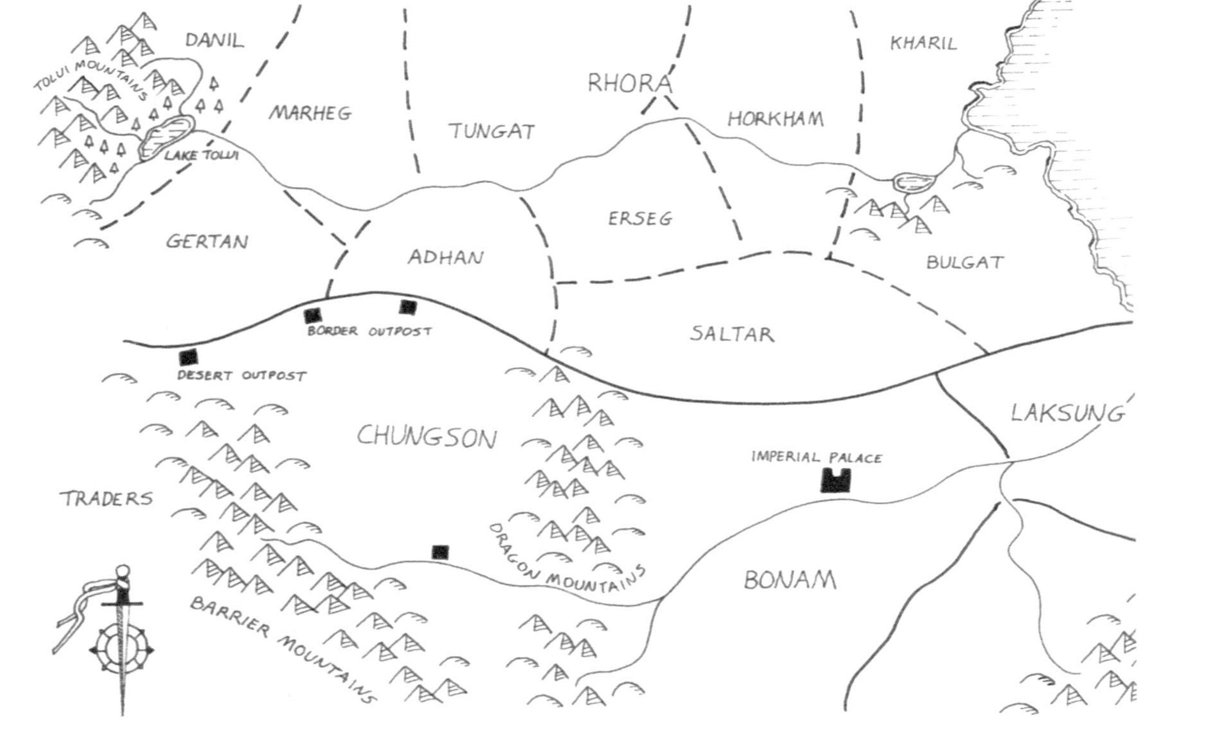

TOLUI MOUNTAINS
DANIL
MARHEG
TUNGAT
RHORA
HORKHAM
KHARIL
LAKE TOWN
GERTAN
ADHAN
ERSEG
BULGAT
BORDER OUTPOST
SALTAR
DESERT OUTPOST
CHUNGSON
IMPERIAL PALACE
LAKSUNG
TRADERS
DRAGON MOUNTAINS
BONAM
BARRIER MOUNTAINS

Chapter 1

Screams echoed around Shuree as she fought for her life. A thick arm swung a sword at her head and she ducked, slicing her attacker across the stomach. He bellowed and stumbled back, one hand over the bloody wound. Shuree flinched, but he'd given her no choice. His tribe had attacked hers. She checked no other raider was near as the Erseg warrior regained his balance. Shuree crouched, ready for his attack.

"Leave," she ordered. She had no desire to kill him, only to stop the fighting, to protect her family and her people. "Take your warriors and go while you still have men alive."

The man stared at her, clutching his stomach, trying to stop the blood flow. All around, men fought from horses and on the ground. Mothers herded their children away from the battle, heading towards the dusky sunrise while other women used bedsheets to smother the yurt fires the raiders had started.

Shuree panted, waiting for the man's decision and scanning for the next threat to her life. She wouldn't die today, despite her compassion. If he attacked her again, she would kill him. A couple of women screamed as they were lifted onto raiders' horses and then someone blew a horn and sounded the retreat.

Her heart lurched and she reached for her bow and an arrow, hoping to save Yesugen and Tegusken, but her quiver was empty. She'd run out long ago. She watched helpless as they kicked and screamed and were ridden out of the camp. Her attacker stumbled back and another raider galloped up to him. The second man was in his mid-twenties and held his sabre aloft, ready, a fresh scar across his cheek. He eyed her warily, his deep brown eyes penetrating, as he hefted his tribe member onto his horse, but she made no move to attack.

How could she stop this endless cycle of violence? "This killing must end," she called. "Surely we can come to some kind of agreement."

His eyes widened and he gave a small nod before he kicked his horse into a gallop and rode away, joining the horde of men escaping north.

Shuree lowered her sabre and sighed. They were gone. For now. But they had crossed a line this time by kidnapping the women. Her skin prickled at the thought of what would happen to gentle Tegusken and her mother, Yesugen.

Amar ran to her side. "Why didn't you kill him?" he demanded.

She looked at her youngest brother. "Because death isn't the answer." She wiped the blood off her blade and sheathed it. "What did they take?"

"I don't know."

Yesugen's youngest daughter sobbed, crumpled on the ground. Shuree hurried over and pulled her into her arms. "It's all right," she soothed. "We'll get them both back."

"They'll kill my mother!" she wailed.

Shuree couldn't disagree, it was a possibility. She glanced for Amar, but he was already in deep discussion with his best friend Gan, who had drawn two lines of blood over his bald skull. He thought they showed his prowess as a warrior, but all she saw was someone who was proud to be a killer.

"Come now." She helped the girl to her feet. "I need you to be brave and gather the rest of your siblings together. The quicker we put the camp back to rights, the faster we can go after your family."

The girl wiped away her tears and tucked the hair that had fallen out of her braid behind her ears. "You will get them back, won't you Shuree?"

"I'll do everything in my power," she promised.

As the girl left, Shuree's best friend, Badma ran up, looking as beautiful as always, her long-sleeved dress unstained by dirt or blood and her black hair shiny. "Are you all right?" She flung her arms around Shuree, with no care for how filthy she might get.

Shuree nodded, hugging her, though her arms ached from the fighting. "How are you?"

"Frightened. Did you see they took Tegusken?"

"Yes." Their friend was such a gentle soul and she would be terrified. She exhaled. "When you've confirmed your family is safe, I need you to help gather the wounded and ask if the healers require assistance." She would figure out how to get the women back.

"Of course."

Shuree passed yurts covered in blood spatter, stopped to help children find their parents, and accompanied the injured to the healers. One woman sobbed over the dead body of her husband and Shuree's heart broke. She knelt beside her. "I'm so sorry."

The woman turned with a fierce expression on her face. "This has to stop. The khan needs to make this fighting stop."

Shuree agreed, but she wasn't sure anything she said could convince her father retaliation wasn't the best course of action. "I will do what I can."

The spiritual advisor, Erhi, approached with two warriors to carry the body away. Shuree left, but everywhere she went women looked at her with pleading eyes or accusation. She was the khan's daughter, the only female warrior and the Tribal Mother. It was her duty to protect and nurture them. The responsibility weighed heavily on her shoulders.

Eventually she arrived at the tent she shared with her father and Amar. Amar jogged up behind her. Shuree pushed aside the tent flap and found her father, Temujin Khan already seated at the head of the table, a deep scowl on his face and clenching his long black plait in front of him as Jambal demanded they go now to rescue his wife and daughter. Next to the khan sat her two eldest brothers, almost identical to their father though their plaits weren't as long, and then around the table sat Temujin's ten advisors, all battle-hardened warriors still wearing the dirt and blood from this morning's battle.

Her father interrupted Jambal and asked Amar, "How many injured?"

"Twenty, and ten dead," Amar answered. Their tribe was getting smaller with each raid.

Temujin sighed. "They took much of our harvest."

So that's what they wanted. Shuree placed some cheese and meat on the table and ensured the men's glasses were full before she poured herself a glass of mare's milk and sat.

"And my wife and daughter!" Jambal shouted. "We must go now!"

"We will have to get both back," Amar said.

"Without the harvest, we won't survive the winter,"

the khan agreed. Jambal opened his mouth and Temujin continued, "We will take the time to extinguish the fires and restock our weapons only. We can attack this afternoon."

He couldn't be serious. They couldn't go on like this. "Fighting isn't solving anything," Shuree argued. "We need to talk to the Erseg tribe, and perhaps we can compromise, trade with them so they don't have to raid."

The men around the table grumbled at her. "We must not show any weakness," one of the advisors said.

The khan nodded. "Daughter, you do not understand. There is no talking to these people."

"Have we tried?" she asked.

"If we do not strike back, they will think us vulnerable and will take advantage," Amar said.

"They must pay for the lives they took, little dragon," her eldest brother, Yul added, his affectionate smile revealing the gap between his two front teeth.

He'd given her the nickname the first time she'd sparred with him. He'd said she was as beautiful as a dragon, and just as dangerous, her sword her fire. She wouldn't let the endearment sway her. Why wouldn't they recognise that fighting wasn't working? "We've been raided by three tribes in the past four moons," she said. "Too many people are dying. We must find a different solution."

"Your brothers are right," Temujin said. "Talking will only show we don't have the men to fight and they will raid us more frequently."

Frustration simmered in her blood. "More die each raid," she said. "Our people are grieving. Continuing on the same path is madness."

Her father's expression darkened. "You have had your say, daughter. Now do your duty as Tribal Mother and visit the families of the dead."

She'd been dismissed. "Yes, Khan." She rose from the table and pushed aside the heavy tent flap, the soft felt not at all soothing.

Outside, she took two deep breaths to calm her anger, but the normally fresh air of the steppes was mingled with smoke and blood, souring her stomach. How could she convince her father and the elders of the Saltar tribe that change was desperately required?

"Shuree, have they made a decision?" Her grandmother, Nergui walked over to her.

"We are to raid them this afternoon."

Nergui's face fell. "Will there be no end to the violence?"

Shuree tucked her arm into her grandmother's and walked her towards Erhi's tent. "Has it always been like this?"

"Yes, but it's getting worse. The interior of the steppes is drying out, and the tribes there are struggling to grow food. They need what we can produce here on the edges in the more fertile areas."

"Has no one tried to trade?"

"There have been times, but then a khan gets greedy and wants more and the fighting starts again."

"I suggested we talk to the Erseg tribe, but no one listened."

"You are a good child." Nergui patted her arm. "You are wise beyond your years, but your father will never listen, not when their people killed his father."

Revenge was a vicious cycle.

They stopped by the spiritual tent. "I must visit the bereaved," Shuree said.

Nergui hugged her. "You are doing well in your role as Tribal Mother since your mother passed."

Her heart twinged. Gone only a year ago and still it

hurt as if it was only yesterday. "Thank you."

She went into the spiritual tent where Erhi prayed over one of the dead warriors. Shuree waited until Erhi finished and opened her eyes. The black circle tattoo under her right eye marking her as their spiritual advisor seemed more prominent today.

"Shuree, I knew you wouldn't be long. Are you ready to visit the families?"

She nodded, though she was never ready. She would rather ride into battle than deal with the grief these families faced. It reminded her too much of her own grief when her mother had died.

"Then let us go."

***

By midday Shuree's head throbbed with the pain of unshed tears, she hurt from the despair of the families, and her muscles had stiffened from the battle. Hopelessness filled her as the warriors gathered their weapons and mounted their horses. They were going to rescue Jambal's family and get their harvest back.

Though Shuree had been trained to fight, she only protected their home, never riding out when the men attacked. Her father called her over. "You are in charge until I return. Your duty is to ensure the camp is fortified and to protect our people."

She raised her eyebrows. How could they fortify the camp when all their warriors rode into battle? There were no fences aside from those around the sheep herds and no easy way to defend the collection of yurts. Still she replied, "Yes, Khan." His strong arms encircled her, a protection and comfort she had always known. She inhaled deeply, his musky scent filling her nose. She didn't want to let go.

"This is the only way to deal with them, child," he

murmured and moved over to his horse.

Yul stopped next to her after saying goodbye to his wife and children. "Don't worry, little dragon. We'll defeat the Erseg and then maybe they will be willing to talk."

She bit her tongue to stop herself from begging him not to go.

The women and children waved the warriors off, almost half their whole tribe, and worry lodged deep in the pit of Shuree's stomach. Her father and three brothers rode into battle, with no guarantee they would return. She swallowed, blinked the tears from her eyes and turned to Erhi. Her concern spiked again at the deep frown on the spiritual advisor's face. "What's wrong?"

Erhi hesitated. "Dzhambul does not ride with them."

The god of war and hunting guaranteed a successful mission if he rode with them. Shuree's skin crawled and she bit her tongue to stop herself from calling them back. "Can you see an end to this fighting?"

"I will consult the Gods." Erhi left and Shuree returned to her now empty yurt. It was usually full of people meeting with the khan or her family coming to visit. Both her eldest brothers had their own families and yurts, but they were always around, learning how to be khan from their father. Now the lack of people felt like a bad omen.

Shuree couldn't stay here. It was too quiet. She wanted to speak with others, discover if they too had had enough of the endless bloodshed.

She headed back outside and towards the section of the camp where the elders lived. On her way she passed a group of children chasing each other. So quick to recover after an attack, because it was part of their normal life.

At the edge of camp a ten-year-old boy stood with his bow and arrow, facing the direction the warriors had gone. "Do you wish you'd gone with them, Sube?" Shuree asked.

"No. I'm standing guard. With all our warriors gone, we must watch for other raiders."

Sadly he was right. The Erseg tribe wasn't the only tribe that attacked, but at least the tribes to the east of them were friendly. "Thank you. I shall send someone to relieve you in an hour."

He nodded, his eyes not leaving the horizon.

One of the elders drove a cart past her and she jolted at the dead bodies in the back. Their hair tied up in top knots identified them as raiders. "Wait," she called. "Where are you taking them?"

"These are Erseg scum," the elder replied. "I'm dumping them on the steppes."

As if they were waste. That wouldn't do. The dead required a proper ceremony to see them safely to the afterlife. If she wanted change, she needed to instigate it. "Don't go yet. I need to speak with Erhi."

She jogged through the camp until she reached Erhi's tent. Their own dead were lined up inside, and prayers had been said over them. They would be buried tomorrow when the warriors returned.

"What worries you, child?" Erhi asked.

Nerves played in her stomach. "Can we bury the Erseg men properly?"

The older woman gaped at her. "Your father said to dump them on the steppes."

"But he didn't say they couldn't have funeral rites."

Erhi pursed her lips.

"They are people like us," Shuree argued. "Wouldn't you want our warriors to be shown the same respect?"

Erhi's lips slowly widened into a smile. "Yes. Let us go now."

Relief filled Shuree as she returned to the cart with Erhi. "Has the hole already been dug?" she asked the elder.

He nodded.

"Then Erhi and I will see they are buried properly."

His mouth dropped open. "You can't mean to give these filthy animals the funeral rites!"

"That is exactly what I aim to do." She climbed onto the driver's bench seat and took the reins from him. "You can help us."

He jumped down from the cart. "I will not!"

She sighed. "Then please tell anyone who is looking for me I will be back shortly."

Erhi climbed up beside her and it didn't take long to find the hole. Shuree and Erhi lifted the legs of the first body and dragged it towards them. It was cold and stiff and when the face came into view, Shuree fought back the urge to wail. He was barely more than a boy, only a few years older than Sube who stood guard. He wouldn't have even grown his first whisker. A carving of a wolf was pinned to his top, probably a good luck charm. Tears ran down her cheeks. Somewhere a mother grieved the loss of her child, a child who she would have tucked into bed only a few years ago.

After they lay the boy in the hole, Erhi stroked Shuree's back. "He is with his gods now. Qadan will take care of him."

She swallowed, not sure it would be much consolation for his mother. She avoided looking at the faces of the rest of the dead, the similarities of their clothing too close to their own warriors. How many Saltar men would be like these and never return home?

When they were all in the ground, Erhi lit a torch and wafted smoke over them, circling the grave three times while praying, sending them to the afterlife with love. "May Qadan guide you and may you ride the steppes endlessly."

They covered the bodies in dirt.

Shuree was filthy by the time they finished, but her mind was calm. She had done the right thing. When she arrived back at camp, she cleaned herself and then made a round of the perimeter. They really were at a disadvantage with the warriors away. She was the only woman who knew how to fight. The communal tasks were still very much divided between men's and women's roles, but she knew of men who hated to fight, and she had wanted to be like her father from a very young age. It was another thing she'd tried to convince her father to change.

Shuree knocked on Maidar's door. Most everyone gathered at her yurt as she had the largest space and lived alone.

"Come in!"

Shuree pushed open the door and, as she'd suspected, a dozen older men and women sat around Maidar's table eating, drinking and doing their tribal tasks like embroidery or fletching arrows.

"Shuree, welcome." Maidar held out her arms and Shuree placed her hands on the elder's gnarled fingers. "What brings you here?"

Shuree smiled. "I am seeking advice."

Maidar beamed. "Then sit. We can all offer advice, but whether it is any good is another matter entirely. Help yourself to food and drink."

Shuree sat on one of the cushions next to the low table and placed a little cheese and meat on her plate. She wasn't at all hungry, but it would be rude not to eat.

"What is it you want to know?" Maidar asked.

Taking a deep breath, Shuree said, "I am worried. I worry the raids are becoming more frequent and more violent; I worry they are now kidnapping our women; I worry our tribe is left undefended when our warriors retaliate; I worry we won't have a tribe left if this continues."

A fletcher looked up and then swore as he cut his finger. The rest of the elders stared at her, the weight of their gaze heavy.

"Do you not trust your father to lead us?" Koke, one of the most senior elders asked.

Shuree's eyes widened. "No, it's not that." Bless the ancestors, she hadn't considered they might see it that way. "I merely wondered whether there may be a different way, something Father hasn't considered, a way we used to do things, a time when there was peace between the tribes."

"You are right to worry." Maidar glared at Koke. "All my children are dead because of the violence." She glanced around the table. "All of us have lost at least one child."

"What would you propose we do?" someone asked.

"Has there ever been a gathering of the ten tribes of Rhora where we've discussed issues and tried to find a solution?" Shuree nibbled on the cheese.

"Yes, about fifty years ago," Koke said. "It was a massacre. The khan and spiritual leaders of each tribe were supposed to meet at Lake Tolui, but the Marheg tribe ambushed them and slaughtered them all."

Shuree felt sick. No wonder the tribes didn't want to talk. She frowned. "Then how is it we have a good relationship with the Bulgat, Kharil and Horkham people?"

Maidar smiled. "It's because of the marriages," she

said. "Before the massacre, your great grandfather married his daughters into those tribes. Afterwards their husbands became khans and they became tribal mothers. They arranged trade between us."

It wasn't something they could do now. She was the only daughter of the khan and she couldn't marry into every other tribe. She shuddered.

"The Erseg tribe did something similar," Koke said. "They have close relationships with the Adhan and Tungat tribes."

Which left the three most western tribes as unknown. "Do you have any suggestions?"

"Don't like the idea of marrying the enemy?" one of the fletchers asked with a grin.

"There are too many to choose from." The Erseg warrior who had collected his comrade popped into her head and she shook the memory away. One day soon her father would arrange a marriage for her. He might have already done so if she hadn't protested against marrying the Bulgat khan's son. He'd been an opinionated, self-aggrandising man who had fortunately offended her father after the match had been proposed. But perhaps a strategic marriage into one of the other tribes would be wise.

And maybe her father could remarry, take a wife from the Adhan or Tungat tribe, and Amar was yet to marry. That would start the process.

"Perhaps after we defeat them in this battle, the Erseg will be willing to talk," Maidar suggested.

They'd shown no willingness before, so why should this time be any different? Shuree pushed away her plate, her food barely touched, and stood, despair still her companion. "Thank you for your time, and for your refreshments. I must arrange a replacement guard for Sube."

She left the tent and strode over to her friend's place. She wanted a guard who was well trained in fighting. "Vachir, are you home?"

"Come in."

Shuree entered and found Vachir fletching a new batch of arrows. He had been injured in the raid and she was glad he had been forbidden from the retaliation. He hated fighting. His crooked grin eased some of her worry. "Tribal Mother, how are you?"

She sighed. "I am worried. How is your wound?"

"Bandaged and aching." He pulled up his top to show the cloth around his stomach.

If the blade had gone much deeper, he would have died and she would have lost the friend who always made her laugh, and her sparring partner. "Are you well enough for guard duty?" she asked.

"The Erseg won't attack again so soon."

"No, but Sube is standing guard in case other tribes attack, and he is a little too young to do so."

Vachir rose. "All right. I'll take my things out to him. Perhaps he can help me fletch."

"Thank you." She helped him carry the equipment over to the boy. "Vachir will help you."

Sube smiled. "Thank you, Tribal Mother."

As she walked back through the camp, Badma hurried over to her, still as beautiful as she had been this morning, though worry creased her face. "Shuree, can you teach me how to fight?"

Shuree blinked and gave her friend her full attention. "Why?"

Tears glistened in Badma's eyes. "I don't want to be kidnapped during the next raid," she said. "I saw you fighting, and I want to be able to defend myself and my sisters if the warriors are busy elsewhere."

It was another way to strengthen her tribe, but there

would be many who wouldn't approve. She had pestered her father for years to learn and had watched all Amar's training sessions, pinching his training sabre whenever she could so she could practise. Eventually her mother and Yul had convinced her father Shuree would be safer if she learnt the correct techniques, but she'd had to train inside, where no one else could see. Men were supposed to protect their women. "All right. Let me get my weapons. Meet me at the training grounds."

"Thank you."

When Shuree arrived at the training grounds a few minutes later, she found a dozen women of all ages waiting for her.

"They all want to learn," Badma said.

Good. Her father had told her to protect the tribe and fortify the camp. This might not be what he had in mind, but it was time for change. "Let's get started."

Chapter 2

Shuree spent several hours training the women how to shoot a bow and arrow quickly and with accuracy. It was the safest thing for them to learn, so they didn't have to get too close to any raiders. Badma had difficulty pulling the bowstring back far enough so the arrow would fly a decent distance. After the third failed attempt to hit the target she huffed. "What am I doing wrong? The warriors make it look easy."

"They've had years of practice," Maidar said, taking the bow from Badma. "I used to watch my husband," she continued, wrapping her gnarled fingers around the bow. "He would never let me try though." She aimed, released the arrow, and it hit the target with a satisfying thunk. She beamed and handed the bow to the next woman. "Not bad for an old nag."

Shuree grinned.

When they finished, she ordered the bow maker to make each woman her own bow, and the fletchers to make more arrows. The next time someone raided their camp, they would have far more fighters to contend with.

The warriors hadn't returned by the time the sun sat low in the sky. Shuree hesitated outside her yurt. It was her duty to prepare dinner for when her father returned, but the thought of food made her nauseous. Something had gone wrong. Though it was bad luck to think such things, she knew it to be true.

How many men had been killed this time?

She wandered over to the edge of the camp to gaze in the direction of the Erseg tribe. In the dusky light, the steppes were empty. She yearned to mount her horse and ride out to find them, but she was in charge of the tribe and couldn't leave.

Vachir joined her. "They should be back by now." His voice seemed loud in the evening quiet.

She nodded. Neither of them needed to voice further concerns.

"Want me to ride out?"

The warriors would view it as a lack of faith in the outcome and the women in the tribe would worry even more. "Not yet."

He placed a hand on her shoulder. "Have faith."

She wanted to, but Erhi's warning echoed in her head. Something moved on the horizon. "What's that?" She shielded her eyes as if it would help her see further.

"Horses," Vachir said. "I'll go greet them. If you hear my horn, they need help." He jogged over to the herd.

Shuree stayed where she was as the riders came closer. In the fading light it was impossible to tell how many or who they were. Vachir galloped towards them and she prayed they were the warriors coming home. They weren't riding fast, so it was unlikely another tribe attacking them.

Vachir reached the riders and a few moments later his horn blasted into the air. She flinched. They needed help.

People ran out of their yurts, frantically looking around. A couple of mothers were already herding their children away. "I need healers!" Shuree yelled. "The warriors are home."

Koke and two other elders ran for their horses, Badma and Maidar hurried to set up the healing tent and still more women gathered around Shuree, looking towards the approaching party, fear on their faces. Her sisters-in-law stood either side of her.

"Can you see who's at the front?" one of them asked.

Shuree shook her head. It should be her father or one of her brothers, but it was too dark to tell. Someone brought a couple of torches to light the way. It seemed to take an age for the warriors to arrive. She scanned the men at the front for her father.

He wasn't there.

All the men were bloody and exhaustion lined their faces. She counted, recognising Amar, but not her father or her other brothers. At least twenty men were missing.

Her chest squeezed. Now was not the time to panic. She helped Jambal from his horse, the devastation on his face all she needed to know they hadn't rescued Yesugen and Tegusken. She took his horse's reins. "Go, clean up."

He left without a word.

"Sube," she called. "Gather your friends and take the warriors' horses back to the herd. Make sure they're well groomed."

Sube ran to do as she asked.

Shuree turned and almost bumped into Amar. She didn't need to ask the question. Grief covered his face and he shook his head. "Father and our brothers didn't make it."

Stabbing shock pierced her and she caught her scream of anguish before it escaped. Her sisters-in-law weren't so restrained. They wailed and Shuree battled the urge to join them, pushing it hard down into her stomach and inhaling long breaths to calm herself. She was Tribal Mother, she had to lead her people. When she was certain she could keep the scream at bay, she said, "See to your men, and then we will hold council."

He nodded.

Shuree stared across the steppes, the final image of them riding away playing in her mind. All she could hear was Yul telling her not to worry. She would never again hear him call her 'little dragon'. She swallowed hard, blinking away tears. She didn't have time to grieve. She was in charge, she had to care for her people, shore up their defences and protect them. It was time for change. This grief would not happen again. She found Vachir. "Gather the elders. I want to speak to them in my yurt."

His eyes were sympathetic. "Yes, Tribal Mother."

The crowd had thinned out. Families who had lost warriors headed back to their homes to mourn. Shuree swallowed hard. It would be her time soon, but not yet. She spotted Erhi. "Please come to my Tribal Council."

The spiritual advisor acknowledged her with a wave. "I'll be right there."

Then Shuree was alone. Darkness hid her and a tear slipped past her defences. She sniffed, wiping it away. Her father had put her in charge until he returned.

And he hadn't returned.

***

Shuree lit the lamps in her yurt and filled the table with food and drink. Though she had no appetite, others might want to eat. Erhi was the first to arrive and she sat by Shuree's side. Then Vachir walked in with the elders and Amar arrived with Jambal.

"Sit, please."

Amar sat at the opposite end of the table to her. Everyone looked at him.

"What happened?" Shuree asked.

"They were ready for us," Amar said. "The moment we attacked they were on us with a consolidated force, surrounding us on all sides. Our khan fought bravely, but even he knew we were outnumbered. He called the retreat and then he was shot. He fell off his horse and I couldn't get to him." He cleared his throat. "We rode hard to escape."

"How many dead?" she asked.

"Twenty-three," the senior warrior answered.

She wanted to weep. "And injured?"

"Fifty," Amar said. "Maybe ten who might die."

She closed her eyes briefly. They could not go on like this. She turned to Vachir. "When this council is over, ensure the healers have all the help they need. Organise a roster through the night."

"Yes, Tribal Mother."

"I want guards stationed all around the camp," she said to Jambal. "We do not know whether the Erseg will attack again."

"We must get Yesugen and Tegusken back!" he shouted.

She softened her tone. "We will. Did you see them?"

He shook his head.

"Wait a second," Amar protested. "What gives you the right to give orders? I'm next in line."

Shuree glared at him. "Father left me in charge until he returned. He is not back." Her voice broke and she swallowed hard. "I am also Tribal Mother. Until we have time to arrange a ceremony, I make the decisions." She glanced at Erhi. "Am I right?"

Erhi nodded.

"Then we need a ceremony in the morning," Amar said. "We will discuss what to do about the Erseg afterwards."

"We're doing that now," Shuree retorted. "Fighting is not the answer."

"We have to get our people and our harvest back," Amar protested.

"We can't afford for anyone else to die." She could see only one sensible option. Her pulse raced at the mere thought of what she was going to suggest, but the tiny nod the Erseg warrior had given her, gave her hope. "Tomorrow I will ride to the Erseg tribe to discuss matters. I will recover the bodies of our fallen and bring them back for burial and I will retrieve Jambal's family."

"They're not going to do what you want because you ask nicely," her brother snarled. "They'll kill you." Fear shone in his eyes, displacing his angry words.

She stared him down. "That may be so, but I must try something different. If I fail, you can choose to kill more of our men in a revenge attack and keep the circle of death spinning." She glanced at the others around the table. "I will take a wagon for the bodies. I want the rest of you to prepare for their burial."

"Do you think that is wise, Shuree?" Erhi asked.

She shook her head. "I know it is not, but we can't continue to do the same thing and hope for a different outcome."

"I don't like it," Amar said.

"I know, brother. But until Erhi confirms you as new khan, I am in charge. Does anyone else have any suggestions?"

They all shook their heads.

"Then we will go on as planned. Now if you'll excuse me, I need to talk to our new widows." She left the yurt. There hadn't been as much argument as she'd expected. Perhaps she wasn't the only one who realised things couldn't continue as they had been.

She exhaled and went into the tent of Altan who had lost her husband and her son to the fighting. Altan sat on the bed, hugging her fourteen-year-old daughter. The yurt was filled with a bitter cleansing smoke so the spirits of the deceased wouldn't want to return and would instead travel into the sky to meet with Qadan, God of Life.

"I am so very sorry for your loss," Shuree said.

They turned to her, the daughter a younger version of her mother and both with reddened eyes and tear-stained cheeks. "Tribal Mother, this has to stop," Altan said. "We keep losing our men."

"I am going to talk to the Erseg tribe tomorrow. I will get their bodies back so we can have a proper burial."

"They won't listen. They'll kill you, or keep you there."

"Maybe." She hugged Altan, who clung to her for a long moment. Altan's daughter sniffed and threw her arms around them both. Shuree's heart ached. "I have asked the council to prepare for the burial. The people will dig their graves tomorrow."

"Thank you, Shuree. May Qadan ride with you."

"If you need anything before I return, talk to Amar or Nergui."

She jolted. Her grandmother. She hadn't seen her yet and she had just lost her son and two grandsons. As a previous Tribal Mother, Nergui would understand

Shuree's commitments, but as soon as Shuree left Altan, she went straight to her grandmother's yurt.

Her grandmother sat at the table, a mug in front of her, and her eyes red rimmed. "I hear you are going to talk to the Erseg." The quaver in her voice brought tears to Shuree's eyes.

She poured herself a drink, her hand shaking, spilling some of the mare's milk.

"I am." She sat next to Nergui and leaned into her as her grandmother stroked her arm. Hot tears ran silently down her face.

"I wish you safe travels," Nergui murmured. "I admire your courage. My son should have never sought revenge."

It didn't matter. He had paid the price. Shuree's body jerked as the tears took over, wrenching the pain from her body. She took deep breaths to control herself. She still had a job to do.

"Let it go, child," her grandmother said. "We can both grieve here. The others can wait a few more minutes for you."

Shuree buried her head in her grandmother's chest and felt her own sobs as they both cried for all they had lost.

After she had cried herself dry, she sat up, wiping her face on her arm sleeve. She sipped her milk and when she was sure she could speak she said, "Should I not return, take care of Amar for me."

Her grandmother nodded as she used her thumbs to wipe away her own tears. "I will."

Shuree kissed her grandmother goodbye and continued to visit the bereaved families. In each yurt she heard the same words: things had to change, people were tired of losing their loved ones. Her sisters-in-law were particularly vocal. They had seven children between them. Shuree prayed talking with the Erseg would work.

She hesitated outside Gan's yurt. She had never liked him, didn't like the way he influenced Amar and had a lust for violence. But his father had died in the raid, and his mother might need comforting. She called out before entering and found Gan pacing the tent, his mother sobbing on the bed surrounded by her other children. Gan whirled to her.

"What is this goat dung I hear? You want to talk to the Erseg killers? They're murderers, barbarians." The hostility in his eyes almost made her step back. Instead she moved towards his mother, keeping an eye on him.

"Thirty-three men have died in the past two days," she said. "We can't afford to lose any more."

Gan spouted vile expletives at her and his mother sat up, wiping her eyes. "You apologise to our Tribal Mother immediately!"

Gan glared at them both and stormed out of the tent without saying a word.

Shuree exhaled.

"I'm sorry, Shuree. He's grieving," his mother said.

"There is no need to apologise." She hugged the woman and then her children. "I am so very sorry for your loss."

"And I am sorry for yours."

She nodded, unable to speak. Grief would consume their tribe if they let it.

It was late before she arrived back at her yurt. Amar sat at the table. "You don't know what you're doing," he said. "You'll be killed." His voice broke and she swallowed hard as grief reared its ugly head again.

"I have to try something, Amar. We can't keep fighting."

"I'll come with you with some of our warriors."

She shook her head. "You can't. Any sign of violence will cause them to attack. If I go, a female alone, they are more likely to listen before they attack."

"I can't lose you too." He stood.

She hugged him. "I'm hoping you won't, brother, but I need you to stay here to protect the tribe." She hesitated and then exhaled. "I also need you to promise me one thing."

He frowned. "What?"

"If I don't return, you can't attack the Erseg again. We need to recover, we need to find a replacement for our harvest and figure out how we will survive the winter. It is not the time to continue fighting."

"I can't promise you that."

"You must." She stepped back, shook his arms. "I go willingly, knowing I might not return. We need to ensure our tribe's survival."

"You ask too much of me." The words sounded as if they were torn from his throat.

"I know. But our tribe needs strong leadership more than they need revenge. Every woman I spoke to is happy I am trying something different."

He was silent for a long moment. "All right. I promise."

Relief filled her. "Thank you. Now I need sleep if I am leaving early in the morning."

She kissed his cheek and went to her sleeping mat. A few minutes later, he extinguished the candle and the yurt fell dark.

"Sleep well, sister."

She smiled. "You too, brother."

Chapter 3

The sun was a hint on the horizon when Shuree gathered her bow and arrows, and her sabre to wear at her side. Amar joined her as she left the tent and they travelled across to the horses in silence. No one else was awake. Her muscles tightened as she fetched the wagon horse and hitched it up while her brother saddled two more horses for Yesugen and Tegusken. After she freed them, they could ride ahead and bring word to the tribe of Shuree's success.

The land was taking shape in the sun's early rays as they finished and Erhi approached them. "I have consulted with the Gods," she said. "Qadan be with you."

Some of Shuree's tension lessened. It was more than her father had had. "Thank you, Erhi." She hugged the older woman and then noticed Nergui coming their way. Shuree wanted to be gone before she had to say goodbye to too many people. She hugged her grandmother tightly. "I will return within a few days." It would take longer to reach the tribe with the wagon and she wasn't certain how long it would take to negotiate with the Erseg.

"May the ancestors ride with you."

Shuree turned to her brother. "Take care of our people."

"I will." He hugged her hard. "Be safe, little dragon."

She nodded and climbed into the wagon, trying to portray an image of confidence. The smooth leather reins were comforting in her hands, though the hard wagon seat was uncomfortable. With a flick of the reins, she was on her way. She didn't look back, even though she knew it might be the last time she saw her family. She needed to be a vision of courage and strength.

But she prayed to Qadan she would return.

***

Late in the day, the Erseg camp loomed ahead of Shuree. From a distance, it looked exactly like her own camp, white yurts arranged in rows, with horses penned on the outskirts. Smoke wafted from the apex of the tents. Women would be preparing dinner for their families. So normal.

Shuree had had time to consider the best way of approaching them and decided to be upfront and honest. Guards stood at the edge of the camp and behind them people went about their daily business. She stopped her wagon in front of the nearest warrior, a middle-aged man with thick, muscled arms and legs and a derisive expression on his face.

"What do you want?" he demanded.

Smiling, she said, "I am Shuree from the Saltar tribe. I have come to gather the bodies of our dead and to retrieve the women you kidnapped."

The man laughed and withdrew his sabre. "You and who else?"

"No one. I wish to negotiate with your khan."

"He won't want to speak to you."

She raised her eyebrows. "You presume to know the wishes of your khan? You must be very close to him." Some of the tribe members watched her warily, others scanned the steppes behind her, and a teenaged boy ran further into the camp, possibly to fetch someone.

The guard glowered at her.

"Please direct me to his tent." She flicked the reins to nudge the horse forward.

He grabbed the horse's harness. "You're not going anywhere."

A woman's scream split the air.

Shuree's heart leapt. That was Jambal's wife. She reacted before she could consider the consequences and leapt from the wagon, grabbing her sabre from her belt. The guard lifted his weapon and she swatted it aside and ran towards the yurt the scream had come from. She burst through the door to find a man towering over Jambal's naked wife, his pants around his ankles, his pale hairy bottom facing Shuree. He spun at the interruption and Shuree shoved him back, getting between him and Yesugen and Tegusken who was cowering behind her mother. She raised her sabre. "These women are not yours."

"Shuree!" Yesugen cried.

"Get dressed," Shuree ordered, her eyes not leaving the man's. "We're going."

The guard from outside stormed in brandishing his sabre.

"Lower your weapon," Shuree said. "I want no trouble here. I have come for my people."

Jambal's family were on their feet behind her, Yesugen pulling on her dress.

"Then you should not have drawn your sabre," the guard said. The other man picked up his weapon from across the room.

The guard stood between them and the door. She didn't want to fight her way out. "Take us to your khan."

"No."

The door flew open and a tall man strode in, his dark eyes hauntingly familiar, the fresh scar on his cheek now healing. "What's going on?"

Relief filled her. Perhaps he would help her. He knew she didn't want violence. "My name is Shuree and I'm from the Saltar tribe. I wish to talk to your khan so I can take my people home."

"She drew her weapon, Dagar" the guard complained. "She attacked us."

"My friends screamed in fear." She kept her gaze roaming over the men in the room. She was outnumbered. "I attacked no one, simply stopped him from hurting another man's wife."

"Put your pants on," Dagar growled at the man who had attacked Yesugen. "The khan will speak with you later."

The man looked a little worried as he dressed.

Dagar turned his attention to Shuree. "I can take you to the khan. Leave your sabre on the table."

She hesitated. "Do you swear by Qadan to offer us safe passage until I have spoken to the khan?"

"I swear."

Hopefully her mercy the other day would offer her some protection.

She lay her sabre on the table and took Yesugen's and Tegusken's hands. "Show us the way."

"Go back to your post," Dagar said to the guard. "See that her wagon doesn't get misplaced."

Shuree nodded her thanks and followed Dagar out of the tent. He was silent as he led them through the camp, the shadows drawing long as the sun sank towards the horizon. Tribesmen, and the occasional woman, stopped to watch them, word having spread about her arrival. Yesugen's hand trembled in hers and Tegusken sobbed quietly. "Be brave," Shuree whispered. "Jambal has been frantic and I hope you will be home to him tomorrow."

"Are they coming to free us?" she whispered.

"No. I will free you."

Nearby some young men stood in a circle cheering around two grappling wrestlers. Just like the young men did back home.

Dagar stopped outside a large yurt in the centre of the camp and pushed open the flap. "Ogodai Khan, you have a visitor." He gestured for them to enter. "This is Shuree from the Saltar tribe. She wishes to speak to you."

Ogodai turned to her. He was a large man, tall and lean, but muscled like a sleek scout horse. His dark hair was tied in a top knot and he wore the tunic and pants of their people, yet his dark cloth was of an excellent, more refined quality. "Are you here to beg for mercy?"

Her muscles tightened as chills raced along her skin. "I am here to put an end to the endless fighting between our tribes."

He laughed. "They send a woman to do a khan's job?"

She straightened her spine. "Our khan left me in charge until he returned, when he attempted to retake the things you stole. He did not return."

Ogodai's eyes widened.

"So I am khan until an official ceremony can be performed. As such, I wish to negotiate with you, and end our hostility."

"What can you possibly offer us?" Ogodai said. "We have your harvest and your women."

This was her only chance. If she couldn't convince him, her people were doomed. "Peace," she said. "Access to our harvest every year and perhaps more, depending on what you want."

He laughed again. "It seems the Saltar tribe is on the verge of capitulating. Do you not have enough men left to fight?"

"Our women are tired of burying their loved ones as I'm sure are yours." She straightened her spine and kept her voice steady. "There is a better way of living which doesn't require constant fear and vigilance."

Dagar shifted, his expression speculative.

The khan yawned and glanced at his nails. "No. You can join the other women as wives for my men."

Shuree's skin crawled. She would have to get past Dagar to leave the yurt and there were no weapons within easy reach. Talking was her best option. She heard Yul's voice in her head. "You can do this, little dragon." She stared at the khan, daring him to back down. "I *will* have what I came for—these women and the bodies of our dead, so that we can send them to the afterlife."

"And what of my men who died raiding your camp?" Ogodai demanded. "They received no such send off."

"They did," Shuree corrected him. "I had them buried north of our camp, facing your land. Our spiritual advisor said the rites. They shouldn't be damned for eternity for following your orders to attack."

Ogodai gaped at her and another man rushed into the tent—the man whose life she spared.

"Father, what's going on?"

The khan's son! Hope filled her as Shuree smiled. "We meet again."

His eyes widened. "You!"

"You know this woman?" Ogodai asked.

The man looked between his father and Dagar. "I fought her during the raid."

"And yet she survived?"

Shuree waited for him to confess. To be beaten by a woman would lose him status.

He glanced at her. "You called the retreat."

"My khan, Shuree bested my brother. She could have killed him, but she spared his life, told him to leave and not return," Dagar said.

He was the khan's son as well? Perhaps she could reason with them.

"This small thing?" Ogodai was horrified.

"I am a warrior as well as a woman," Shuree said. "Though I do not enjoy killing, I will in order to save my people. There was no need to murder your son when you were retreating."

He pressed his lips together. "We owe you a life," he said. "Choose one woman to take with you."

She shook her head. "I will take both women and my dead," she said. "Or I shall tell all who will listen that I bested the khan's son."

Ogodai narrowed his eyes. After a long moment he nodded once. "Very well. Your dead are piled on the steppes to the west. Speak to no one of the mercy you gave."

Relief filled her. "Thank you, khan." But that wasn't all she'd come here for. "Afterwards, can we discuss peace between our tribes?"

Ogodai frowned. "I will think on it. See me before you leave."

She inclined her head. "Thank you."

She smiled at the two brothers and they stood aside so she could exit. She took the women's hands and led them out of the tent.

"Are we really safe to leave?" Yesugen asked.

"It appears so." But the khan could change his mind, so they must make haste. She strode through the camp towards the wagon. The sun had disappeared beneath the horizon and the light was fading. The same man stood guard and he scowled at her.

"The khan has given us permission to gather our dead," she told him.

He glanced behind her. "Fine."

Shuree looked over her shoulder. Dagar had followed them. He would ensure the khan's wishes were carried out. She helped the women into the wagon noting her bow and quiver of arrows in the back. "I will return after I have my men."

He shook his head. "I will show you the way."

Her shoulders tensed. Could he be trusted? "You may ride one of our horses."

"It might be faster if I walked."

His humour made her smile. The Erseg horses were of a higher quality than the Saltar breed and were highly sought after by the other tribes for their stamina and build. "Suit yourself."

Though it was dark, it did not take long to find the pile of bodies. A couple of wolves lurked nearby and Shuree shot them.

"We should go," Tegusken whispered, casting a fearful glance at Dagar. "This is a trick. They won't let us go."

"I will see my father returned to his land," Shuree said. "If you wish to go, you may take one of the horses and ride home."

Yesugen clucked her tongue. "We will help. You cannot lift the bodies by yourself."

The smell of dead flesh reached them and Shuree gagged. She hadn't considered that the bodies had been in the sun all day. She gritted her teeth, glad of the dark. "Tie your sash over your nose." It might help a little.

She dismounted and studied the pile. Her skin prickled as she made out an arm or a leg sticking out. Her brothers and father were there. Her knees buckled and she fought to stay standing. Grief battered her and she took a moment so she could speak calmly. "Yesugen, can you take the feet?" She wanted to be gone from here as soon as possible.

Tegusken vomited nearby and her sobs were loud in the night. "Tegusken, move upwind until you can't smell it anymore." She would be of no use, but Shuree envied that she didn't have to stay here with this.

She picked up the cold, stiff shoulders of the nearest man, refusing to examine the body. She didn't want to see who it was. Yesugen took the feet. "On the count of three." She counted and they lifted, but Yesugen struggled with the weight. They managed to heft the body into the back, but it wasn't easy. At least she didn't have to worry about hurting them.

Yesugen bent over, panting. At this rate, it would take them hours to lift the remaining twenty-two bodies.

"Let me help." Dagar's deep voice startled her. She'd forgotten he was there.

"Thank you." She placed a hand on Yesugen's shoulder. "Join your daughter." She approached the next body.

"Let me take the shoulders," Dagar said. "They're heavier."

She went to the feet, relieved she wasn't near their

faces. If she saw her family, she wasn't sure she would be able to keep going.

They worked quickly, lifting body after body into the back of the wagon, and she kept count, to ensure they had them all. Shuree forced herself not to think about what she was doing, to simply lift and carry, breathing through her mouth to avoid the smell. Her muscles ached and it was with relief she reached twenty-two. Only one more to go.

She turned back to the ground and frowned. What was the round lump next to the body?

She moved closer and crouched down, and horror spiked her. A head. Her gaze went to the body and she recognised the cut of the tunic. Her father. She stumbled away and vomited, grief and disgust overwhelming her. She fell to her knees, sobs wracking her body. It wasn't bad enough that they'd killed him, they'd mutilated him as well. Beheadings were reserved for only the worst crimes and Amar had said their father had been shot.

"Shuree?" Yesugen touched her shoulder.

"It's Father," she sobbed. "They cut off his head."

Yesugen gasped. "Child, I'm so sorry."

Her chest spasmed and it was almost impossible to get enough air.

"We will ensure he goes to the great steppes in the sky." Yesugen stroked her back. "Because of you, he will be saved."

Shuree struggled to inhale slowly. Yesugen was right. She had to take back control, had to finish what she had come here for. It still took her a few minutes before she managed to control her shaking. She wiped the tears from her eyes and stood. With another deep breath, she turned. Dagar stood by the body, waiting for her.

Swallowing hard, she moved over.

"I am very sorry," he murmured. "I did not know. I will find out who did this and punish them."

She didn't respond as fury replaced the grief. It was just as well Dagar had taken her sabre from her because she wanted to pave a path of destruction through the Erseg camp for the way they'd mutilated her father's body.

"Shuree? Are you ready?"

She jolted at Dagar's voice and unclenched her fists, taking a moment to calm the anger. Violence wasn't the answer.

In front of her lay her father. She gritted her teeth and took hold of his legs, lifting him into the wagon. Squeezing her eyes closed to stop the tears from leaking out, she turned back to where the head lay. Carefully she cradled it in her arms, brushing the hair away from his face. They had cut his plait as well, the hair he hadn't cut since he was a boy, and now it fell loose around his cheeks. Gently she lay her father's head next to his body. She touched her fingers to her lips and then brushed his cold ones. She would never hear his commanding tones again, never be comforted in his strong arms.

She tied the back of the wagon in place and covered the bodies with a blanket. She wiped her eyes and turned to Jambal's family. "You two start back to camp." She cleared her throat to stop the rasping. "Tell Amar I am negotiating with the khan and I will return in a couple of days. Hold the funerals without me."

"He might not let you go," Yesugen said, glancing at Dagar. "You should come with us."

"I promised I would return," she said. "If I don't keep my word, they will never trust us." She hugged both women. "I will be fine. Make sure my brother knows not to come for me."

Yesugen nodded. "I wish you all the support of our ancestors."

"I will do my best to ensure she is safely returned to you," Dagar said.

Hope filled her.

Yesugen and Tegusken both got onto the wagon, the spare horse tied to the back, and rode away. Shuree didn't mount her horse. She would walk next to Dagar. "Let's go."

***

A different guard waited at the edge of the tribe and when he recognised Dagar, he waved them through.

Shuree focused on her surroundings. It was close to midnight and fatigue hovered around her like a swarm of flies. She stroked her horse's nose to calm herself as she followed Dagar through the camp to the horse herd at the edge. It was unsettling how familiar the setting was. She could almost be in her own camp if it wasn't for the unease swirling in her belly. They were all Rhoran tribes, so why were they constantly at war with each other?

"You can leave your horse here for the night." He showed her where she could stow her tack.

"Is your father willing to talk to me?"

"I cannot speak for him. He will see you in the morning."

Her muscles tightened. "And in the meantime?"

"I would like to hear what you have to say. You can stay in our guest yurt."

"Will I get my sabre back?" She'd left her bow in the wagon.

He nodded. "When you leave."

So Dagar thought she'd be allowed to leave. She

unsaddled her horse, brushing it and then taking the tack into the nearby yurt, conscious of Dagar's gaze on her. Though nothing in his body language was threatening, her shoulder blades itched. Experience told her the Erseg couldn't be trusted, but Dagar hadn't sent anyone after Jambal's family, so perhaps he was a man of his word.

When she was finished, she followed him into a yurt on the edge of the camp. A lantern glowed and she blinked a couple of times to get used to its brightness. The yurt was much like their guest yurt with a mattress to one side and a low table with cushions surrounding it on the other. Dried meat and cheese were on the table, along with a bowl of water, some clothes and a washcloth. A couple of storage chests were against the curved wall.

"I requested the yurt be prepared," he said. "I will wait outside while you clean yourself."

"Thank you." She waited until he left before she examined herself. Her clothes were stained with blood and other bodily fluids and her hands were filthy. She washed her hands and face first, trying to rid herself of the stench. Then she quickly stripped and washed the rest of her body, before she dressed in the dress and pants. They felt wonderful and were the same style as she had at home, only the embroidery was a little different. She tied her dirty clothes into a bundle and then fetched Dagar who stood outside the yurt.

"Can I wash my clothes somewhere?" she asked.

"I will get someone to do that for you," he said. "Place them by the door and I'll take them when I leave." He moved back inside, his presence filling the room. His dark eyes studied her and made her skin prickle. The intensity was terrifying and thrilling at the same time.

She sat at the table across from him and chose a piece of cheese from the platter. Her stomach was a little unsettled, but she hadn't eaten in hours and she needed the energy. She also needed to keep control of this conversation. "Why are you willing to listen to me?"

He smiled, just a slight upturn of his mouth, but it made him so much more attractive. "I am grateful you didn't kill my brother. I have no desire to be khan."

She raised her eyebrows, willing her heartbeat under control. "I thought every man wanted to be in charge."

"And I thought every woman wanted to tend her family."

She raised her cup in acknowledgement. Perhaps together they could convince others that peace was the way forward. "My tribe is my family," she said. "I want them safe and happy. Will you tell me why you raided us? Was it simply for the harvest or was your aim the women as well?"

"The women were unexpected," Dagar said. "Father was not impressed."

"And yet he did not return them."

"To do so would appear weak."

Always the concern for how they appeared to others. It was exhausting. "Do you not have many women in your tribe?" She hadn't seen many walking around.

"Tell me what you propose for peace," he said.

The trust wasn't there yet. She would have to offer her information before he would offer any, but she would do so gladly, if it prevented anyone else from feeling this hollow ache inside. "I am not certain," she admitted. "I don't know what you want, so therefore I am not sure what to offer. I just know I can't keep seeing my people die." Her voice broke and she took a moment. Her hand was steady as she poured mare's milk into her cup and filled his as well. Focus on the future, on what her tribe needed. "You do not have the fertile land to grow crops, but your horses are much stronger than ours. Perhaps we can trade some of our harvest for some of your horses each year." Yul would have loved to have an Erseg horse.

"Is that it?"

"What else do you want?" Frustration tried to push its way into her tone and she exhaled. "Part of the problem is, we only come together to fight, we do not know each other." Her mind whirled for other options. "Perhaps you can join our summer hunt next year. We meet with the Kharil, Horkham and Bulgat tribes each year. We trade and talk, and our young people flirt and find marriage matches."

He frowned. "Wouldn't that be an opportunity to attack us? You would be at strength and we would be vulnerable. How can we trust you?"

The first step was always the hardest. Each side worried about betrayal. "Don't you have treaties with the Adhan and Tungat tribes? Perhaps they can come as well. We can all trade and learn about each other."

He chuckled. "Do you know how optimistic that is? The tribes of Rhora are warriors not poets."

Dagar was right. But there were still so many similarities between them. She remembered the wrestlers she'd seen earlier. "Then how about a tournament? Our people can compete for prestige; we could have archery tournaments, wrestling bouts, horse races. The winning tribe gets a title until the following year."

"There's still the trust issue." He sipped his drink.

Why did she have to do all the work? Didn't he have any suggestions of his own? "So we camp at a distance from each other and our khans and spiritual advisors gather at a central point to lay down rules for weapons and behaviour."

"You're determined to make this work, aren't you?"

She nodded. "The women of my tribe are tired of grieving. There must be another way. We are all Rhoran."

"We are," he agreed and stood. "I will let you rest. There will be a guard at your door."

Of course. "As long as he doesn't enter, he will be safe."

His lips twitched. "As long as you don't try to leave, you will be safe." He left.

Shuree exhaled and slumped over the table. It had gone better than she had expected. If Dagar had his father's ear, perhaps they could negotiate a peace. Though his brother may not like it. Maybe she should have allowed Amar to come with her. As a male, he might have been given more respect, but he also had more of a temper.

She finished her drink and carried the lantern over to the mattress. She checked beneath the covers for any surprises and then scanned the tent for anything else she might have missed. Only the single entrance to monitor. Without any weapon, she felt naked, but she'd worked with Vachir to sharpen her hand to hand combat skills.

And she desperately needed to sleep so she was alert tomorrow.

It was her turn to trust Dagar's word.

She lay down and fell asleep.

Chapter 4

Shuree woke as the sounds of the camp entered her yurt. People called morning greetings, horses whinnied in the distance and children shrieked with laughter. Suddenly she sat bolt upright. This wasn't her yurt.

Memories flooded back. She was in the Erseg camp, awaiting discussions with the khan. Her pulse slowed. Had Yesugen and Tegusken made it home yet? Would Amar keep his promise to wait until she returned? He would be furious when he saw what they'd done to their father. Her stomach heaved at the memory.

No, she would remember him as he had been, strong and kind. Some nights she would wake and listen to him speak with her mother about things that were troubling him, how to always do right by the tribe. He never showed that vulnerable side to anyone but his wife and Shuree. She used to climb into his lap when she was little and cuddle him, tell him everything would be all right.

How she missed him already.

She brushed the tears from her cheeks and stood, stretching her aching muscles, and brushing the wrinkles out of the clothes the best she could. It was important she spoke to Ogodai soon, before her brother had time to retaliate for their father's mutilation. She took a piece of dried meat from the table and opened the chests she'd noticed the night before. One had a hair comb in it, so she undid her plait and combed her hair before rebraiding it. She was as presentable as she could be.

She pulled down the top flap of the yurt which let smoke out when the central fire was lit. The light was still soft, pale, so perhaps not long after sunrise.

Ogodai might not be awake yet, but she should let the guard know she was.

As she approached the door, it rippled and a voice called, "Are you awake, Shuree?"

She stopped where she was and said, "Yes, come in."

Dagar ducked his head as he entered. "I wasn't sure if you would still be sleeping." He stood upright, his clothes tidy, no sign of fatigue on him, yet he'd probably had less sleep than her. He adjusted his top knot and smiled, then winced as the scar on his face pulled.

She sympathised with his pain. "I am ready to speak to the khan."

"How about we break the fast first?" He gestured for her to leave the yurt.

"Thank you." Shuree hoped his courtesy was genuine. She walked with Dagar to a nearby tent. Inside were his brother, a young woman and two girls. Dagar's brother glanced up and scowled. "What's she doing here?"

She glanced at Dagar.

"Having breakfast with us." Dagar turned to her. "Shuree, this is my brother, Batbayar, his wife, Narangerel and his daughters, Naran and Saran." He gestured for her to sit. "Shuree is from the Saltar tribe, here to speak with our khan about peace."

Narangerel smiled. "Welcome. May your journey be fruitful."

Batbayar gaped at his wife. "What are you saying?"

She glanced at him. "I am tired of fearing for your life every time you ride out," she said. "I want my children to have their father."

Excitement hummed under Shuree's skin. "I understand. I hope the khan and I can come to an agreement."

Narangerel pursed her lips. "Perhaps we can talk in private before you see him."

Batbayar was spluttering now. "You can't do that. She's our prisoner."

Shuree stiffened. "I thought I was your guest."

"You are." Dagar sat next to her and handed her a bowl of curd. "You have Shuree to thank for sparing your husband's life at the last raid," he said to Narangerel. "She could have killed him, but she let him go instead."

Narangerel's eyes widened and she reached across the table to squeeze Shuree's hand. "Thank you! Your mercy means the world to me and my children."

Joy filled her. Here was the proof she'd made the right decision. "You are most welcome."

"If I may ask," Narangerel said. "Why didn't you kill him? They attacked you."

"Killing each other isn't the answer," she said. "I know each of the raiders will return to a camp like ours and their wives will celebrate their return. I've seen too often the heartbreak when someone doesn't return." Her chest squeezed as the image of her father's mutilated body flashed before her. She swallowed. "I am Tribal Mother to my people," she said. "And I am currently in charge of my tribe. My duty is to protect and nurture them anyway I can."

Understanding shone in Narangerel's eyes. "If there's anything I can do to help you bring peace, please tell me."

"Enough!" Batbayar said.

Shuree ignored him. "Perhaps if there are others in your tribe who feel the way you do, it would help to voice those concerns to your khan. The more people who speak up about change, the better chance it will occur."

"I will speak to the other women. I know many feel the same as I do." Narangerel glanced at her husband. "Sit down, Batbayar. I've told you I hate the fighting. If I can prevent it, I will."

The children had been silent until now, watching with wide eyes. Saran spoke up. "I would like you to stop fighting too, Father."

"Me too," Naran said.

Batbayar studied them both and his bluster deflated. "You talk about making us weak."

"It takes far more strength to lower your weapons and talk, than it does to swing a sabre," Shuree said.

He glared at her and she sipped her drink. If both the khan's sons could be convinced, would they help her to convince the khan as well?

Naran tugged on her mother's sleeve. "Does this mean they'll stop eating babies?"

Shuree laughed. "We don't eat babies."

"My friend said you did."

"Well your friend is wrong," Shuree told her. "The Saltar tribe is much like the Erseg tribe," she said. "We live in yurts like you, we eat curd and dried meats, our young men wrestle like yours do. We simply live closer to the mountains and share our border with the country

Bonam in the south which means we have more fertile ground. We grow crops in the summer and raise sheep. Our people are craftsmen, warriors, healers and teachers, just like yours."

"But women aren't warriors and you said you fought Father."

"Most women aren't warriors, but my father was khan and allowed me to learn. I have…" Her chest constricted and she corrected herself. "*Had* three brothers and I used to watch them train and wanted to learn. Finally I convinced them to teach me." She smiled as she remembered the lessons. "I only fight when our camp is raided." As would the other women she was teaching.

"Can I learn to fight, Father?" Saran asked.

He frowned. "There is no need."

"There might be if we don't have peace," Narangerel said. "Our girls are vulnerable during any attack."

Perhaps this was another way to convince him. "Two of our women were kidnapped during the last raid," she pointed out. "When your daughters are older, that could easily be them."

He clenched his jaw and sat. "I would die before I would let anyone take my girls."

"That might be, but your death might not stop it from happening." Was she pushing him too far? Surely he had to realise what could happen if the warfare continued. She glanced at Dagar and he gave an almost imperceptible nod. Maybe this was why he'd brought her here.

Narangerel sat back and stared at her husband with horror. "You allowed the men to kidnap women?"

"I didn't know about it until we got back to camp. Father is dealing with those responsible."

"Where are they now? We must set them free."

"They are already on their way back to my tribe," Shuree said. "Ogodai agreed to free them and let us take our dead home to be properly buried."

"Good." She glared at Batbayar. "I expect you to tell the warriors it is not acceptable. We might not have enough women, but that doesn't excuse such behaviour."

Shuree sat forward. "Why don't you have enough women?"

Dagar stood. "It is time to meet with the khan."

Shuree ignored him and waited for Narangerel to answer. "Part of our agreement with the Tungat and Adhan tribes is to allow our young girls to be wedded to their young men."

"But surely you receive young women in return."

She shook her head. "Neither tribe has many women to spare. People say the gods realise we need warriors to fight, so they don't gift us with many girls."

And the Saltar tribe had far more women than men. It was another negotiating point. If more marriages occurred between the tribes, it would make them less inclined to attack each other. Dagar walked around to her side of the table and she stood. "Thank you for breakfast, and for your time. I hope we meet again."

Narangerel smiled. "As do I."

Both Dagar and Batbayar accompanied her to the khan's tent. Her mind whirled with what she could offer, not only the Erseg tribe, but the Tungat and Adhan as well. And if she could reach peace with them, could she reach out to the furthest tribes and also negotiate peace there?

She entered the tent and froze. With the exception of an older woman sitting next to Ogodai, the rest of the people around the table were men, all of them armed. They turned to her and their conversation fell silent. On the other side of Ogodai sat a man with a circle tattoo under his right eye, the spiritual advisor.

Nerves tickled her skin, but she relaxed her shoulders and bowed her head slightly. "Thank you for your time, Ogodai Khan."

He grunted and gestured for her to sit at the opposite end of the table. His sons sat on either side of her. Having Dagar next to her was a comfort. He might stop any rash actions from the suspicious elders. She must choose her words carefully, so as not to offend them. Half the men glared at her as if she was goat dung, though a couple gazed at her as if she was simply an oddity.

The spiritual advisor spoke. "You gathered your dead?"

"Yes, thank you for your permission, Khan. I sent Jambal's wife and daughter home with the wagon, and our spiritual advisor will ensure they are properly buried."

"You say you buried our fallen," the man continued.

"That's right. Erhi said the rites over them and we sent them on their way. I can show you where they are buried if they have family who wish to visit them."

"Why?" one man demanded.

She frowned. "Why show you?"

"Why bury them? We attacked you."

"You did, but these men were following the khan's orders. I always hoped our men who died while fighting were given the same respect."

A couple of men glanced at each other but said nothing. She recognised the squinty-eyed one as the man who had had his pants down when she'd rescued Yesugen and Tegusken.

"Thank you," the spiritual advisor said. "I would like to visit their burial place."

"You are welcome to return with me when I go," Shuree said.

Ogodai raised an eyebrow. "Who said you were going?"

She swallowed but kept her expression calm. "I am sure we can come up with an arrangement."

The understanding in the older woman's eyes reminded Shuree of her grandmother. "I am sure you are right. My son is a reasonable man." Ogodai glared at her, but she paid him no notice. It appeared it wasn't just Narangerel who was tired of the fighting. Shuree relaxed further.

"Would it help if I tell you what Saltar wants?" she asked. "You can decide whether you want the same."

Ogodai gestured for her to go ahead.

"We want peace," she said. "I want my tribe to live without fear of attack and for them to prosper. I want to have good, healthy relationships with our neighbouring tribes, and reach the stage where we willingly share information and skills so we can all grow and prosper together."

One man coughed. "Impossible."

"Why?" she demanded. "It will take trust, but if we all agree to it, then we can achieve it." Men murmured to their neighbours. She was losing them. She needed to speak about concrete actions. "You want our harvest and we could do with stronger horses. We can trade, rather than fight for them."

One man nodded.

"What about your women?" the squinty-eyed man spoke up.

She stiffened. "Our women are not commodities to be traded," she said. "I will never allow them to be forced." She stared at him, and he looked away first. Exhaling, she turned her attention to Ogodai. "However, I can see the benefit of marriage between our tribes. I propose a yearly summer gathering. We can invite all tribes and we can mingle, hold competitions and get to know each other. If you can win the heart of one of our women, then marriage can be discussed."

"A gathering won't work," Ogodai said. "All it would take is one wrong word and fighting would ensue."

He was right. Sometimes it was difficult to stop fights amongst the young men in a single tribe. "Then we set rules," Shuree said. "No weapons at the gathering place. If fights occur, they will be with fists not blades which will reduce the chance of death."

"What kind of competitions do you speak of?" Ogodai's mother asked.

"We have some amazing craftspeople," she replied. "Our embroiderers and saddle makers can show their wares and people can vote on a winner. Perhaps we can have horse races and wrestling matches so our warriors can let off energy."

Ogodai's mother nodded. "That is sensible."

"Who can guarantee such a thing?" Ogodai asked.

"The khans," she replied. "If we cannot control our tribe members, then we should not be in charge."

His face went red.

Her mind spun with options, but perhaps she was letting herself get carried away. She hadn't convinced the Erseg tribe of peace yet, but what if they could find peace for the whole of Rhora? She caught Ogodai's eye. "This is bigger than our two tribes," she said. "I know our allies to the east want the fighting to end. Perhaps we should gather all ten tribes to bring about peace to our land."

"Where would we meet?" someone asked.

The spiritual advisor spoke. "I shall ask the Gods."

A wise idea.

Ogodai finally spoke. "We have much to discuss. Dagar, take her back to her tent."

Surprise had her sit back. Had she said enough, or too much? She longed to keep pressing, but it would only get their backs up. She smiled at the khan before she left the tent with Dagar. His silent presence next to her soothed her. As they walked through the camp, a couple of men glared and put their hands on their sabres. "Will your tribe agree?" Shuree asked.

He glanced at her, concern on his face. "I do not know. Will your brother comply with any agreement we make when he is khan?"

Act confident. "I believe so, but the longer I take negotiating, the less faith he will have that I am safe."

Dagar nodded. "I will do what I can to see you back to your camp today."

"Thank you." She smiled and his serious gaze captured hers, sending a zing through her body. Lowering her head, she ducked into her tent without another word.

When she was sure she was alone, she put a hand to her heart. Now wasn't the time to be attracted to anyone. She had to be focused, arrange peace for her people and not get emotionally involved with a man who could be her enemy.

His courtesy and interest simply lined up with hers. They were trying to improve the lives of both their tribes, reaching for a common goal.

She sat at the table, itching for some embroidery, or something to do with her hands, something which would keep her busy until the khan had made his decision.

But there was nothing.
She sighed and settled in for a long wait.

Chapter 5

It was mid-afternoon before Dagar returned. Shuree had tried to sleep, but Dagar's question about her brother looped around her mind. Would Amar honour her agreement? She had to believe he would decide this was the best course, but seeing their father's dismembered body might spur him to action. Hopefully, her brother was occupied burying the dead Yesugen and Tegusken had returned. Maybe Erhi or Nergui could talk some sense into him. If not, then she had at best another day before they would attack the Erseg.

Her skin prickled. Please, ancestors, give him patience. Don't let him ruin this.

"Shuree?" Dagar's call outside the tent was a welcome distraction. When she opened the door, the expression on his face gave nothing away.

"Has the council decided?"

He nodded. "Come with me."

Her chest tightened. This was it. As she walked back through the camp, her hands were clenched and she relaxed them. Whatever happened, she had done her best. She was proud of that.

Ogodai's tent was still full of the same people. She stood at the end of the table and inclined her head at the khan. Dagar stood next to her.

"Your proposal has opened many old wounds," Ogodai said. "We have lived in distrust of our southern neighbours for so long, it is difficult to overcome it."

She waited.

"Many of my people believe your proposal is a trap, but more of them agree it is time to stop fighting."

Hope stole her breath and she met Ogodai's grave expression. He wasn't happy and the concern for his people was clear. She felt the same way.

"So we agree to a temporary truce," he said. "We feel it is best not to risk antagonising the other tribes by agreeing to peace with only the Saltar tribe. We believe your suggestion of gathering all ten khans together is the best outcome. Our spiritual advisor, Mengu has spoken with the Gods and they have proposed the Dragon Mountains as the meeting place as it is neutral ground, not part of any tribe. We will meet in the low meadow on the night of the full moon, two moons hence. Each khan may bring their spiritual advisor and five warriors. We must start slow, engender trust, before we meet in any large numbers. We will contact the Adhan and Tungat tribes and you will contact the tribes to the east. To the tribes to the far west, we will both send messengers."

Ogodai wasn't after discussion. If she didn't agree, they would refuse any further talks. Fortunately, it was a good proposal, though members of her tribe would argue it might leave them vulnerable to attack while the khan was gone. "Agreed. I will return to my tribe to inform them and then we will contact the other tribes. Should we perhaps send our messengers together to the tribes in the far west? That way they will see the truce is already working."

"A good suggestion," Ogodai said. "I will send three riders as well as Dagar and our spiritual advisor with you."

She blinked in surprise, but pleasure filled her. Showing her people the Erseg were so similar to them would hopefully help them accept the proposal. "When do we leave?"

"First light."

Would it be soon enough? But suggesting her brother might not obey her commands would lead to more distrust. She smiled. "Thank you for this opportunity."

He scowled. "You will come to the communal dinner."

She wasn't sure whether he disliked negotiating with a female, or whether it was because she was Saltar, but it didn't matter. They were getting somewhere. "I would be honoured."

He glanced at his son. "Take her to the campfire."

Dagar took hold of her arm and his light touch sent a shiver through her. When they stepped outside, he asked, "Are you happy?"

"I am optimistic," she said. "We have a long way to go, and the other tribes may not agree with us, but it is a good start." She glanced at him. "How do you feel about it?"

"I am pleased. When will you send word to the tribes to the east?"

She bit her lip. They only met with them once a year, and they had their gathering last moon. It would take time to reach them and she couldn't send a simple messenger to them. It had to be someone who agreed with the gathering and who could convince them to come. "I will send some trusted men as soon as I return." She wanted to go herself, but it would be wise to stay close to her brother.

"My father has ordered me to stay by your side until we reach the gathering."

It was the only way to gain their trust, but she wished it didn't send such a thrill through her.

"And I will get you a better horse so you can keep up with us."

She smiled. "Thank you. Could my tribe have three more for the messengers I send to the eastern tribes?" They would be faster.

"I will speak to Father about it." Dagar stopped walking and faced her. "I told the khan about what happened to your father's body."

She stiffened.

"He will find out who did it and punish them. He has also spoken to those who kidnapped your women. They will not do it again." His expression was fierce.

"Thank you." There would always be people who broke the law and as much as she wanted to demand vengeance, peace was more important.

The communal campfire was on the south side of the camp. A number of people were already there, monitoring the sheep roasting on spits over the flames. Dagar introduced her to a small woman who had a grey streak through the front of her hair.

The woman beamed at her. "Welcome, Tribal Mother. Narangerel told me what you proposed. You have given so many of us hope when we thought there was none."

Shuree's heart filled. "Thank you. I am pleased others feel the same as I do."

"Sit here and I'll get you something to drink. You are our guest of honour tonight."

Shuree glanced at Dagar and he nodded.

Another woman approached, twisting her hands together as she walked. Her eyes were red and her face splotchy. She'd been grieving.

"I heard you gave our dead a proper burial," she said.

"That's right. Our spiritual advisor said the rites and we buried the bodies together."

Tears glistened in the woman's eyes and she said, "Did you see my boy? He wore a carving of a wolf on his vest."

Pain twisted inside her and she quickly got to her feet. "I did. I am so very sorry. He rides now with Qadan."

Tears ran down the mother's face and Shuree opened her arms as she would for any of her own tribe. The woman fell into them, sobbing. "Thank you. He was too young. He never should have gone."

Determination filled Shuree. These deaths had to stop.

Even if she had to travel alone to each tribe and speak to them, she would bring peace to Rhora.

***

"This horse is for you." Dagar led a chestnut horse over to where Shuree was saddling her own horse.

She sucked in a breath. The animal was two hands taller than her own, its glossy coat begging to be stroked. She ran a hand down its withers and felt the strong muscles underneath. It was made for speed and distance. "Thank you. She's beautiful."

"Leave your horse here. I'll get someone to return it to your camp in a few days, but it won't keep up with us and time is of the essence."

It was. Even now her brother could be saddling his own horse to mount an attack. Shuree adjusted her sabre strapped to her waist, and mounted. The sun's rays were peeking above the horizon. Dagar, Mengu, and three other riders rode out of the camp with her, along with extra horses for the Saltar messengers. They rode hard across the steppes, faster than Shuree had ridden before. The Erseg horses were indeed superior to their own.

By late morning, the Saltar camp appeared in front of them. Home. She swallowed the lump in her throat as she spotted children gathering horse dung for fires, and women beating wool to make felt. Such normal everyday activities. Shuree pulled up her horse and the others followed suit. She pointed to the west. "Your people are buried over there, but first we should go into camp so I can introduce you. I don't want to have any incidents."

They continued at a slower pace, until they reached the outskirts where a guard waited. Shuree grinned. "Greetings, Vachir."

Relief flooded her friend's face and his crooked grin was full of joy. "Shuree! I'm so glad you're back." He eyed the others. "Who have you brought with you?"

"This is Dagar, son of Ogodai Khan, and Mengu, the spiritual advisor of the Erseg tribe." She introduced the messengers as well.

Vachir's eyes widened. "Then I guess you had some success. Welcome. Your brother is in the khan's tent."

Shuree raised her eyebrows. "Has there been a ceremony?"

"Only the burial ceremony for the men Jambal's family brought back." He glanced at the Erseg men again and lowered his voice. "Amar was furious about your father's body. He's trying to convince the others to ignore your instructions and seek revenge."

A quiet growl from Dagar and she held up a hand,

her heart pounding. She hadn't come this far to fail now. "I will find him immediately." She turned to Dagar. "All of you, stick close to me. I'm sure this can be sorted out. Vachir, come with us. There is no need to fear an attack from the Erseg."

Vachir followed them to the horse area and Shuree called over some youths. "Vachir, stay here with the Erseg messengers. Help them with the horses and then find them some food." She turned to the youths. "Spread the word I have returned with some of the Erseg tribe. Tell everyone they are our honoured guests and under my protection."

The youths nodded. "Yes, Tribal Mother."

Shuree gestured to Dagar and Mengu and led them through the camp, greeting people as she went.

Sube ran up, his training sabre held out front as he glared at the men. "Do you need protection, Shuree?"

She smiled. "No, Sube, but thank you for the offer. These men are my guests. Could you tell my grandmother I've returned?"

His suspicion was clear in the way he looked them up and down and then ran off with her message.

"Your warriors are young," Dagar commented.

"Sube has a big heart."

"Shuree!" Badma's excited shriek caused Shuree to turn, but she didn't have a chance to prepare herself before Badma flung her arms around her, forcing her to stumble back a step. "You're alive!"

Shuree chuckled, hugging her friend. "I am and I have brought guests from the Erseg tribe."

Badma stepped back and noticed Dagar. Fear crossed her face and Shuree squeezed her hand. "They are friends. I will tell you all about it later. Could you find Erhi for me? Ask her to come to the khan's tent."

Her friend left, turning back a few times as if to

check Shuree was indeed all right.

"You are popular," Dagar commented.

"They are merely surprised." She smiled. "I'm not sure anyone believed I would return."

He grunted.

At the khan's tent she paused. She had to convince her brother to agree with the terms she'd negotiated. She was sure he would insist on holding the khan ceremony immediately. She pushed the flap open. Inside her brother sat at the head of the table and next to him sat the council, including Erhi.

Amar's mouth dropped open. "Shuree!"

"Greetings brother. Permit me to introduce Dagar, son of Ogodai Khan, and spiritual advisor, Mengu from the Erseg tribe." She turned to Dagar, but before she could continue her introductions, her brother stood, outrage turning his face red.

"They mutilated our khan! They need to die." He reached for his sabre.

Dagar went for his weapon and Shuree stepped in front of him, heart pounding, holding up her hands in pacification. "Drop your weapon, Amar! These are my honoured guests and you will treat them as such."

"They are murderers," he growled, ignoring her command and moving closer.

Shuree drew her own sabre and held it out. "You will not touch them." Her gaze flicked to the men around the table. "Jambal, restrain my brother."

Jambal hesitated.

"As your Tribal Mother, I order you to restrain him. If it weren't for me, you would not have your family back."

Jambal stood and Amar glared at him.

She did not want bloodshed. "Amar, I will ask you only once more. If you disobey me, I will banish you from this tribe." The words tore at her throat, but it was the only way she could get him to understand how serious she was.

He gaped at her and lowered his sabre a touch, but it was enough for Jambal to disarm him.

"Sit back down," she ordered. "All of you, place your weapons on the floor behind you."

So many startled looks and one man opened his mouth to protest. "Now!" Shuree insisted.

They did as she requested and her pulse slowed. She turned to Dagar. "My apologies for this poor welcome. I can only imagine my brother's grief made him forget himself."

Dagar nodded, but he watched the table warily.

Shuree continued the introductions. "Next to Amar is our spiritual advisor, Erhi."

Erhi stood and walked over, greeting the newcomers with outstretched hands. "Welcome. I am pleased to meet you finally." She smiled at Mengu. "Would you like refreshments first, or would you like to see where we buried your dead?"

"Refreshments would be appreciated," Mengu replied.

Shuree gathered the weapons the warriors had discarded and placed them in a pile out of reach of the table. While she did so, Erhi made the council shift to make room for them.

Shuree gestured for Dagar and Mengu to sit either side of her. "We have much to discuss," she began. "As you will know from Yesugen's and Tegusken's safe arrival home, the Erseg tribe were willing to negotiate with me."

"Thank you, Mother," Jambal said. "I did not think I would see them again."

She smiled. "Vachir tells me our warriors have been

buried."

"Yesterday," Amar answered. "We gave Father and all our warriors a proper send off." The look he gave Dagar suggested he wanted to send him to the other side as well.

Her chest squeezed. She would have liked to have been able to say her goodbyes to her family. She swallowed.

"It truly pained me to discover what someone did to your khan," Dagar spoke, his tone low. "Please know it is not the normal way for my tribe. My father is investigating it."

Clearing the lump from her throat, Shuree continued. "I have discussed our circumstances with Ogodai Khan and we have come to a temporary truce. Dagar has come to help me implement it."

His brother frowned. "And if we don't like it?"

"You don't have to like it, you just need to obey it." Shuree's tone was hard. She hadn't risked her life and come this far for her brother to mess it up.

"Tomorrow I will be khan."

Several men nodded in agreement.

Erhi cleared her throat. "That is not necessarily the case."

Shuree jolted and everyone turned to the spiritual advisor.

"The law states a khan's child must be the next khan, but it doesn't state whether that child be first born, or male, or female." Her expression was slightly apologetic. "If there is a disagreement on who rules, the tribe may vote."

Shuree sat back, her mind whirling. She'd never even considered it. "I don't want to be khan."

Amar unclenched his fists. "Then we don't have a problem."

Beside her Dagar shifted and he looked deeply uncomfortable. If Amar didn't agree with her proposal, he could ruin everything. "The agreement with the Erseg tribe is contingent on all the tribes of Rhora."

A few men gaped at her and one said, "You can't decide that."

She held up a hand to stop the murmuring. "No. That is why the truce holds until after the gathering of all Rhoran khans in two moons' time." She explained the terms. "We both hope to set up trade and better relations between the tribes."

Amar glared at her. "It would never work. They are likely to attack us the moment our backs are turned."

"My father has given his word," Dagar growled. "He will not go back on it."

"Says you. All we know of him is he attacks us, mutilates the dead, and steals our women."

Shuree spoke before Dagar could retort. "That is why it is so important we hold this gathering." She glanced at Erhi. "Mengu says the Gods have chosen the Dragon Mountains as the meeting place."

Erhi inclined her head. "A good choice."

"We won't have to worry about the dragons?" Jambal asked.

Shuree looked at Erhi to answer. "I believe they reside in the upper reaches of the mountains. They should have no interest in what we do."

"The dragons don't matter. We have not agreed to go," Amar said.

"We have," Shuree corrected him. "I negotiated in good faith as leader of the Saltar tribe. I expect you to respect my wishes."

"A woman knows nothing of war," one of the men said.

"We are not discussing war," she replied. "We are

discussing peace."

"We should not have these discussions with them here." Amar jerked his head towards Dagar and Mengu.

"Dagar is here as my guest. He needs to be involved in all our discussions so he may grow to trust us. We must be open and honest about our plans. His tribe is taking as big a risk as ours in doing this."

Amar stood. "I am in charge here."

Shuree stiffened. "No, you are not, brother. Not yet."

Amar looked at Erhi who said, "Your sister is right. She is acting khan until the ceremony."

"Then we continue this discussion when I am khan."

Her gut swirled like a dust storm. She couldn't let this fall apart. Too much was at stake. Her father's last words echoed in her mind. It was her duty to protect their people. Though it was the last thing she wanted, she straightened her spine. "Our people can vote on our next khan."

As Amar gaped at her, she said to Erhi, "I will stand up to be khan. What do I need to do?"

Chapter 6

Shuree showed Dagar to the guest yurt. The uproar that had ensued after her announcement still had her head spinning, but Amar was right about one thing—Dagar didn't need to witness siblings fighting. Erhi had calmed Amar and then taken Mengu out to the buried Erseg with the Erseg messengers and some warriors Shuree trusted to protect them.

"I thought you were speaking with the authority of your tribe when you came to us," Dagar said as they reached the door.

"I was. My brother agreed to my proposal before I left. I fear he is still mourning my father and brothers, particularly after what happened to Father."

He sighed. "I should warn my tribe."

She placed a hand on his arm. "Please wait. This afternoon we will vote in our new leader. If Amar is chosen, you and your people can ride home and warn them."

"I trusted you."

The concern and betrayal in his eyes twisted her heart. "And I trusted my brother." Her chest ached. So close to a peaceful solution. "I will talk to him again. I need to make him see sense."

"He will tell you what you want to hear in order to become khan."

He was right. She closed her eyes and exhaled. "Then I will still put my name forward."

"Even though you don't want to be khan?"

She nodded. "Peace for the whole of Rhora is far more important than my own desires."

His hand brushed her chin as he lifted it and she opened her eyes. "That is brave. Fighting with family is far harder than with anyone else."

He understood. "I'm sure your brother wasn't happy with you when you mentioned I'd bested him on the battlefield."

"No, he wasn't." Dagar chuckled. "I will wait until this evening before I leave," he said. "Not because I trust your people, but because I believe in you. If anyone can bring peace to Rhora, it is you." He walked into the yurt.

Shuree's heart beat uncomfortably hard in her chest. With one last look at Dagar's door, she went to find her brother.

Amar was still in the khan's tent, and Gan was with him when she walked in. They both glared at her and Amar's fierce hatred stabbed her, but she would not let her love for him sway her. He had always been quick to react, to fight and then forgive and he was easily swayed by his friend. As children they had often bickered and because she hated it so much, she usually gave in. Not this time.

"I need to speak with my brother alone, Gan."

"You're going to slaughter our tribe," Gan said as he shoved past her and out of the tent.

Shuree ignored him, instead meeting her brother's

gaze. "Don't look at me like that, Amar. You know why I went to the Erseg tribe."

"How can you even consider peace with them?" he demanded. "They cut off Father's head."

Nausea rose in her and she blocked the memory. "I know. I found him." Her voice was dull.

He stood and came to her, wrapping her in his arms. He wore the same musky scent as all the men in her family and she squeezed her eyes closed, breathing through her mouth so it wouldn't affect her so much. His voice switched to cajoling. "Don't you see what barbarians they are? They don't treat the dead with any respect." The tone was so familiar from their childhood arguments.

She wanted to cling to him and sob, but she wouldn't let him distract or persuade her. She stepped back, swallowed hard. "Dagar says they are investigating it."

Amar frowned. "Well he would say that."

She shook her head. "I believe him. He wants this peace as well. It was he who told the khan I spared his son during their raid. It was my compassion that ensured Jambal's family were freed and we recovered our bodies." She had to make him understand. "Their camp is so much like ours," she continued. "Their traditions the same. I stayed in a guest yurt and when I woke, the sounds outside were like being at home. I spoke with many of their people at dinner and they all want peace, but not all trust us to keep our end of the bargain."

He scowled.

"See, brother, without talking to them, we wouldn't have known. We would have reacted emotionally instead of rationally. Our warriors become fewer with every battle. Soon there will be no one to protect us."

"But you've seen to that as well, haven't you?" Amar said. "You're training the women to fight."

"To protect themselves and the tribe," she corrected. "We can't rely on our warriors any longer. We need to take control of our own safety."

He turned away. "You are our mother's daughter," he said. "Strong and wilful."

Shuree took it as a compliment. "Thank you."

"You put us in a very vulnerable position," he said. "This gathering could lead to the destruction of our tribe."

"Or it could be the beginning of a stronger community," she responded. "The old ways aren't working, brother. Surely you can see that."

He sighed. "I don't agree with you, but we will let our tribe decide. Erhi wants us both to explain our vision of the future and then the tribe will choose who they want to lead them."

It was fair. "I will accept what they decide, but if you should win, I ask that you let the Erseg men go free and that you arrange your own discussion with Ogodai."

"I will free the Erseg men, but I won't guarantee to speak with Ogodai." His expression hardened.

It was the best she could hope for. She'd pushed her brother far enough. "Thank you."

Someone called to them and Shuree opened the door to find Erhi outside the yurt. "It is time."

Shuree squeezed her brother's hand. "No matter what happens, know I love you, brother."

He smiled for the first time. "And I love you."

Nerves swirled around Shuree's stomach as she went to fetch Dagar. Would her people agree with what she was trying to achieve? She couldn't remember any stories of a female khan. She stopped outside the guest yurt. If all her promises to Ogodai were broken, the Erseg would never trust the Saltar again.

Taking a breath, she called, "Dagar, would you like to witness the voting?"

The tent flap swung open and he stepped out. "Yes."

He said nothing as they strode to where the tribe had gathered by the communal fire. Erhi stood on a platform in front of the crowd and Amar stood next to her. "Wait with your people." Shuree pointed to his other tribe members who stood with Vachir and Badma.

Before she could join her brother on the platform, an old, wrinkled hand grabbed her arm. "Shuree."

A lump lodged in her throat as her grandmother hugged her.

"I'm pleased you are back." She lowered her voice. "The women support you. You will make a strong khan." The confidence in Nergui's voice gave Shuree strength.

"Thank you." She stepped up next to her brother and Erhi called for silence.

"Our khan, Temujin died during the raid of the Erseg tribe," she began. "Custom normally has the leadership passing to the eldest son, however this is not law. The law dictates that any of the khan's children may be khan and as such Shuree and Amar have both indicated a desire for the role. They will each speak and then you will decide who you wish to lead our tribe." She indicated for Shuree to begin.

Shuree cleared her throat. "After our khan died, I travelled to the Erseg tribe to retrieve our warriors' bodies, and to free Yesugen and Tegusken who had been taken during the raid," she said. "My goal was to see our people were returned safely to our land, but I also hoped for change." She scanned the crowd. Jambal appeared unhappy as Gan whispered in his ear. Then Gan rubbed his bald head and smirked at her, the hostility in his gaze making her skin prickle. Maidar and Koke stood next to her grandmother and their smiles gave Shuree hope.

"For decades the tribes of Rhora have fought each other, stolen harvests and horses, flocks and women. We have lost so many men in battle and our numbers decrease. And yet we have a respectful relationship with the tribes to our east. Why can't we have the same relationship with the other tribes?"

One of her sisters-in-law nodded and the other shushed her baby who had begun to cry. Shuree was doing this for them, and all the others like Altan and her daughter, who now had to live without their husbands and sons.

"I spoke to Ogodai Khan while I was with the Erseg. I proposed peace and he was reluctant. Trust is the rarest jewel. We discussed many options such as a yearly gathering like we do with the eastern tribes, holding games and competitions, banning weapons so tempers and misunderstandings can't turn deadly. But in the end we realised we must start small, with a group of people who can make decisions for their tribes and sign a peace treaty. Ogodai agreed to my suggestion of gathering the ten Rhoran khans together to discuss a permanent peace treaty and proposed a two-moon truce. The Gods have told us to meet in the Dragon Mountains to the south and should I be your khan, I will meet with the other Rhoran leaders and broker a peace between our tribes."

She indicated Dagar in front of her. "Dagar is the son of Ogodai. He travels with me to show their commitment to the process. My goal is to stop the fighting and to live in peace with each other, trading goods freely and sharing our skills." She scanned the crowd. Some of the warriors were stony-faced, but others appeared interested. She wasn't certain she had said enough to convince them. Stepping back, she indicated for Amar to speak.

"My sister is young and naive," he said. "Though her goal is worthy, we cannot trust these people. If the khans gather, it will be slaughter with the Erseg tribe triumphing and ruling us all. We must stand firm, we must train hard and be vigilant against their attack. We cannot be weak. The Erseg tribe desecrated our khan's body and left our people to rot on the steppes. They are not worthy of our trust."

Below her Dagar shifted, a deep scowl on his face. Some of the warriors nodded along with Amar's speech.

When he was finished, Erhi spoke. "Trust is a precious gift," she said. "Not easily given. Perhaps it would be wise to hear from Dagar, to find out what the Erseg truly want."

Shuree squirmed. They hadn't discussed this. Dagar covered his surprise quickly as Maidar called, "Let him talk."

Amar's face was a thundercloud as Erhi gestured Dagar onto the stage. Dagar glanced at Shuree and she held out a hand to help him up. "Tell us how your tribe feels about the fighting."

He stepped onto the centre of the platform. "Greetings," he said. "I don't feel it is my place to stand here, speaking to you when you are choosing your new khan, but I am honoured you want to hear more about my tribe."

Hope rose in her. It was exactly the way to get her

people onside.

"I will be honest with you, as Shuree was honest with us. Like you, there are members of my tribe who do not trust. They fear being overrun and that fear blinds them. When I asked them what they truly want it is peace, but they can't see a way to get it. Shuree has offered us a way, by talking with us, by being vulnerable, by risking travelling to our tribe when she knew she may not be welcome. Her courage impressed my father, Ogodai Khan. He saw her strength and was humbled by it. We too fear someone will use the gathering of the khans as an opportunity to attack, to take control, but we can't let fear rule us. Our spiritual advisor asked the Gods and they support the meeting, they suggested the neutral ground of the Dragon Mountains. I can only believe the Gods too want to see us at peace." He stepped down.

Shuree's chest was so full of hope she could barely breathe.

Erhi spoke. "I too have communed with our Gods," she said. "They told me the same as they told Mengu. The Dragon Mountains is where we will find peace and strengthen our people." She gestured to Amar and Shuree. "And now we must choose our khan. Shuree and Amar, please turn your backs to the tribe."

Shuree glanced at her brother as she turned. His lips were a thin line, his eyes staring at a spot across the steppes. What was he thinking?

"If you support Shuree as khan, please step to your left," Erhi said. "If you support Amar as khan, please move to your right."

Murmuring ensued as their tribe members chose with their feet. Shuree's muscles were tight as she waited. She would be graceful if she was defeated, though she wasn't sure how she would face Dagar. He and his tribe had trusted her.

"What are you doing?" a man growled.

"I can choose whomever I want," a woman answered.

Shuree winced. She hadn't considered that families would have different opinions. She hoped relationships would not be strained. Perhaps they should have arranged for a secret vote somehow.

The wait seemed to take forever. She didn't dare look to her brother or Dagar to gauge their reactions. She itched to tap her feet or her fingers, but it would show how nervous she was and her people needed to see only her strength. She would find out if her gamble had paid off soon enough.

Finally, Erhi said, "The vote has been counted and verified by Nergui and Mengu. You may intermingle again."

Of course. If they stayed where they were, she and Amar would know which way they had voted when they turned around. It was another few minutes before Erhi said, "Amar and Shuree, you may face the tribe."

Shuree turned and looked at Erhi rather than her tribe. She wasn't certain she wanted to see their expressions.

"The tribe has voted," Erhi announced. "Our people have chosen their new khan. Will you both abide by your tribe's will?"

"I will," Shuree and Amar answered.

Erhi smiled. "Then please step forward..." She paused and Shuree held her breath. "Shuree Khan."

Air exploded from her and her head spun. They had voted for her? They agreed with her vision of the future? Tears welled in her eyes as she stumbled forward. Amar steadied her.

"Congratulations, sister," he said. "I pray you are

truly right to trust them." He hugged her and then stepped off the platform to join the rest of the tribe.

Erhi gestured for Mengu to join her on the stage to help with the ceremony. Shuree couldn't move, could barely believe this was happening. Amar was right. She was young. Being khan was more than negotiating peace. She would have to lead the tribe afterwards. Panic threatened to overcome her and she spotted Nergui hugging Amar and then they both turned to her and the faith in their eyes calmed some of the anxiety. She scanned the crowd and met more excited expressions as well as a few warriors who were not impressed. Finally her eyes met Dagar's. He winked at her, but the relief on his face had to be a mirror of her own.

"Today we welcome a new khan to lead us," Erhi began. "And in the spirit of what we are trying to achieve, Mengu, the spiritual advisor of the Erseg tribe, will help me with this ceremony. Step forward, Shuree."

Shuree did so.

"Our khan is our leader, our guide and our servant. She must always make decisions for the tribe based on what we need now and in the future." Erhi turned to her. "Shuree, do you promise to lead us, guide us and serve us, today and into the future?"

Her nerves settled and determination filled her. "I promise."

"The Gods bless this appointment. Drink now to seal your promise." Mengu handed her the ceremonial bowl full of litak.

The liquid burned down her throat and made her head spin.

"Please welcome your new khan, Shuree."

The tribe cheered and Shuree smiled, still finding it difficult to comprehend. They had so much faith in her.

She couldn't let them down. The weight of responsibility landed on her shoulders, heavy and uncomfortable. She held up a hand and the cheers quietened.

"Thank you for this honour," she said. "There is much we need to do to prepare for peace. I would like to meet with the council now and then we shall announce our way forward." She stepped off the platform towards Dagar. "Come with me."

The crowd parted to let her through, many slapping her on the shoulder or wishing her luck. So much hope on people's faces. She had to deliver.

Raised voices to her right caught her attention. Gan yelled at Amar, but she couldn't make out the words. Amar glanced around, caught her eye and then turned back to Gan, shaking his head and leading him further away from the rest of the tribe.

What was Gan trying now? The tribe had decided. He knew his opinion was in the minority. She sighed and continued through the camp, hoping Amar could talk some sense into his friend.

At the door to her father's yurt she hesitated. It was truly hers now. Would he be proud of what she had done? She sighed and went inside and offered Dagar a drink.

"You are overwhelmed," he said.

"I wasn't certain they would support me."

He smiled. "You know your people's wishes better than you think. The majority supported you. They want change as well."

She had no words.

"What will you do now?"

"We need to contact the other tribes," she said. "Send them an invitation to the gathering."

Erhi entered the tent and with her were Mengu and

the members of the council. Amar paused just inside the door and Shuree gestured him in. "You are still a member of the council, brother."

"Thank you."

They sat around the table and Shuree took a moment before she sat in her father's seat at the head. No, it was her seat now. She rested her forearms on the smooth wood, the same way her father had done whenever he sat there. She would do him proud.

"We must focus on the gathering of the khans," she began. "I need to send trusted riders to our allies in the east and invite them."

"I can ask the Gods who to choose," Erhi said.

A good idea. That way she wouldn't have to worry about sending someone who disagreed with what they were attempting. "Three riders will also join the Erseg messengers and travel to the far western tribes. We do not know how they will react, but we hope that seeing the two tribes cooperating will give them hope and not fear."

"What do we do in the meantime?" Amar asked.

"We need to prepare for winter," she said. "With our harvest reduced, we must ensure we have enough food. I suggest we send people to Bonam and trade our sheep for their rice."

"We wouldn't have to do it, if the Erseg hadn't stolen our food," one man grumbled. "Surely they should give it back as a sign of good faith."

"My father has sent a half dozen horses with us," Dagar said. "They will allow you to reach the other tribes faster, and you may keep them when your riders return."

It was a generous arrangement and the man fell silent.

"Who will go to the Dragon Mountains with you?"

Amar asked.

She was allowed five warriors. She would have to choose those with cool heads who were slow to anger. "I will think on it," she said. "If you have suggestions, I would welcome them."

They discussed the direction of the tribe and it was night by the time they were done. Shuree stood. "Thank you for your advice and comments. We shall prepare our riders to leave at first light tomorrow, but now I believe it is time to eat."

A communal meal had been organised to celebrate the new khan.

"There is one more thing we need to do," Erhi said. "With you as khan, we must fill the role of Tribal Mother." She frowned. "No, I guess it would be Tribal Father in this case."

Shuree blinked. The role normally went to the spouse of the khan and when her mother had died, it had fallen to her. But she had no spouse or children. That left Amar as her only male relative. "Amar will you be Tribal Father until I marry?"

He smiled. "I would be honoured."

"We shall hold the ceremony tonight by the fire."

She gestured for the council to leave the tent but couldn't stop the lingering doubt. Would Amar follow her lead and support the gathering after she left? Or would Gan convince him his way was better?

Chapter 7

Over the next few days, Shuree was forced to calm many prickly tempers. The warriors didn't like Dagar walking around the village, so Shuree made sure he stayed close to her. The other Erseg men had already left to take messages to the far western tribes and Mengu spent his days with Erhi. To keep Amar busy, Shuree gave him the task of arranging the supplies to trade with Bonam. She hoped it would keep him away from Gan, but every time she saw Amar, Gan was right by his side.

To counteract the hostilities, she made sure Dagar spent time with each group in the tribe so they could get to know him. This truce was far too delicate to leave to chance.

At night they sat by the communal fire and answered any questions from her tribe. Three evenings after Shuree had become khan, Maidar brought her lute out to play. Others soon joined and the music flowed around them.

"Do you play?" Shuree asked Dagar.

He shook his head. "My brother does, but I never learnt." He was quiet a moment, watching those around the flickering firelight. "We play these songs in my tribe. I could be back home."

She squeezed his hand briefly. "I saw so many similarities when I visited you. We are one people, simply separated into ten tribes."

"I thank Qadan that you came to us. This," he waved his hand at the people around the fire, "is a much nicer way to live."

Shuree had no words as he turned his gaze back to her. An unfamiliar warmth filled her. "I thank Qadan you didn't kill me the moment I stepped into camp," she replied, smiling to keep the sting out of her words.

"I promised my father I would send him updates," Dagar said. "Would one of your men take a message for me? I hope hearing from me will lessen his concerns about the khan gathering."

"Of course. I'll ask Vachir to take it. Send updates whenever you like."

"Thank you."

Around them children were dancing, pulling up a few adults to join them. Maidar's seven-year-old granddaughter ran over to them and held out both of her hands to Dagar. "Can you dance?"

Shuree's mouth dropped open as Dagar took the girl's hand. "Not very well, but I will try for you."

They joined the dancers and the other adults nodded a greeting at Dagar. He danced well, moving with grace and a hypnotic rhythm. As the beat changed, he picked up the little girl and swung her around, and her shrieks of glee were all the music Shuree needed.

She scanned those who still sat around the fire. All eyes were on Dagar as he danced and reluctant respect shone in their eyes. Maidar made a gesture towards the pair and grinned slyly at her. She had put her granddaughter up to it.

That didn't matter. What mattered was they were making progress.

The next day while Shuree was introducing Dagar to the fletchers, Badma approached.

"Shuree, are you going to continue to teach us how to fight?"

Dagar glanced at Shuree in surprise. "What?"

She inwardly winced. "After the raid, the women wanted to learn how to defend themselves," she told him. "They were upset about Yesugen and Tegusken being kidnapped and wanted to ensure they weren't taken during the next raid." She turned to Badma. "With the truce in place and the khan meeting only two moons away, is it necessary?"

"Yes, it gave us confidence," she said. "The Erseg tribe isn't the only tribe that has raided and we haven't heard back from the others yet. We'd like to be prepared."

Shuree couldn't argue with that. "All right. I have some time now. Can you gather the others?"

Badma grinned. "We'll meet you at the training grounds." She ran off.

"Do your women not trust their men to protect them?" Dagar asked as they walked back to the khan's tent so she could gather her weapons.

"It's not that." How could she explain? "Knowing I can protect myself gives me strength. I can protect my grandmother and any children nearby, freeing the warriors to fight those who attack us. I don't like feeling helpless or reliant on others."

"I can't imagine you ever being helpless," he said.

A flush of warmth spread through her. Dagar knew all the right things to say. Many of the single men in the tribe had seen her as a way to get closer to the khan, and not as a woman in her own right. Though perhaps that was Dagar's aim too. Now she was khan, he would have a position of power as Tribal Father if she was to marry him.

Her face heated. Not that she was thinking about him in that way. He was simply an attractive man who was being kind to her. The silence grew between them and she had to say something. "Thank you."

"Your people have a lot of faith in you. They want peace as much as you do. It surprised my father and brother to discover how many others in our tribe agreed with you."

She entered her yurt. "Did it surprise you?"

"Yes. My whole focus was on protecting my people. It didn't occur to me there might be a better way." He studied her. "I'm glad there is."

"Me too." She strapped her sabre to her belt and then retrieved her quiver of arrows and her bow. "Do you want to find Mengu?"

"I'd like to watch you teach."

His presence would be a distraction, but she could deal with it. "This way."

Across the camp, the group of women Shuree had taught last time had grown. Amar and Gan wandered over with a couple of their friends.

"Are you trying to get all the women to take on men's roles now, Shuree?" Gan ran a hand over his bald head and then adjusted the sabre at his waist.

Engaging him would only rile him further, so she ignored him.

"We'll continue with shooting today," she said. "The bow maker is making you all your own bows, but these are built for men, so they may be a little tricky to draw back initially." She demonstrated how to hold the bow and notch the arrow. "Sight the target and pull back." She released her arrow and hit the bullseye.

They had three targets to work with, so the women lined up and took turns. Shuree monitored their grip and aim, correcting their position, offering suggestions for improvements. Some couldn't pull the arrow back far enough so it had enough speed to hit the target, and some of the women's aim was off.

Gan laughed and plucked some grass off his dark tunic. "They're terrifying. I'm shaking in my boots." His sarcasm was clear and Badma flinched.

"Ignore him," Shuree said as she corrected her friend's elbow. "You will improve."

Dagar stepped forward. "May I help teach? You can't correct everyone at once."

She smiled. "That would be great. Thank you." She stepped back so he could help Badma and went to the next woman.

"What's he doing?" Gan exclaimed.

"Helping," Shuree replied. "Which is what you could do rather than stand there being insulting."

"You've turned into one of them, haven't you?" Gan demanded. "A couple of nights in the Erseg tribe and now you think they're better. Did you hump all of them or just him?"

Amar leapt to his feet, fury on his face and Dagar spun around, his fists clenched.

Shuree held up a hand to stop them from responding and stalked over to Gan. "I've had enough of your attitude. Give me your sabre."

The man glared at her.

"I am your khan and you will obey me."

He glanced around as if looking for support and found none. Slowly he undid his sabre belt and handed it to her.

"Now you can help the children gather horse dung

for the fires." At the look of absolute outrage on his face, she continued, "When you stop acting like a child, I'll stop treating you like one. Now go. I want to see what you have gathered when I finish here."

She waited, heart racing, until he shifted and then strode away, muttering curses under his breath. She exhaled quietly and then turned back to the woman she'd been helping. "Shall we continue?"

***

Later that afternoon Shuree left Dagar talking with their horse master. She wasn't sure how much Dagar could tell him about why the Erseg horses were so much stronger and faster, but she liked that he tried.

She needed to find Amar and speak to him about Gan. Vachir intercepted her, concern covering his face.

"Gan has been trying to convince the warriors that Amar would make a better khan."

She sighed. "Are many listening?"

"Mostly his friends. Some tell him to be patient because they don't believe you'll return from the khan gathering alive."

Surprise made her laugh. "Well, that would certainly solve the problem."

Vachir grabbed her hand. "Don't laugh. I heard someone suggest they kill Dagar which would stop the Erseg from wanting peace."

Goat dung. "Thank you for telling me. I was on my way to speak to Amar. Will you keep an eye on Dagar? He's with the horses."

Vachir nodded. "Good luck."

She was going to need it. She found her brother sitting at the table in their tent, a drink in front of him. "We need to talk about Gan."

He looked up at her and sighed.

"Did you know he's trying to convince the warriors you would be a better khan?"

"I can't stop him voicing his opinions," Amar replied, shifting in his seat.

"But you can tell him you're not interested."

"You want me to lie to my best friend?"

Shuree stepped back, shocked. "You still want to be khan?"

Amar shrugged and played with the cup in front of him.

"Amar, talk to me. This is serious. The fate of our people lies in communication, trust and peace." She sat next to him and placed a hand on his shoulder.

He shifted away. "It hurts," he said. "That everyone chose you and not me."

Her heart went out to him. "They didn't choose me, they chose peace. If you had offered it, they would have chosen you."

"You can't guarantee peace."

"No, but I can guarantee I'll try. Our people want change." An idea popped into her head. "Have you visited the families of the grieving yet?"

"You did that."

"It's not a one-off thing, Amar. As Tribal Father you need to continue to nurture them. It has been almost a week since the raids. Go to them, see how they are coping, find out if they need anything and talk to them about what they want."

"I wouldn't know what to say."

"None of us do. Take Nergui with you. She will be able to help."

He sighed. "All right."

If that didn't change his mind about fighting, she didn't know what would. "Amar, you need to talk to Gan. He's also been suggesting someone kill Dagar."

The surprise in his eyes soothed her. "What?"

"He sees it as a way of ruining our truce. You need to talk him out of it, or at the very least, keep a close eye on him."

"I will." He sipped his drink. "Gan was ropeable when he overheard the girls talking about the way Dagar danced last night." He rolled his eyes. "A few want to marry him."

Unwelcome jealousy surged through her and she forced a smile. "Then our attempts at peace may still work." She touched his arm again. "I really need your support, Amar. The gathering of the khans is a turning point, but we need to get there first."

Amar gave her a small smile. "All right, little dragon. You've convinced me. I'll keep Gan in check."

Her heart squeezed as he hugged her.

She hoped he was telling the truth.

***

A quarter moon later, Vachir ran up to Shuree as she was heading for the training ground with Dagar.

"Shuree." He placed his hands on his knees and panted before pointing to the east. "Riders are coming."

She exchanged a glance with Dagar and they moved as one to the outskirts of the camp. Perhaps half a dozen riders moving at a trot towards the camp. Around her warriors gathered with their weapons ready.

"There is no need to panic," she called. They were probably members of the Bulgat or Horkham tribes. "Shall we ride out to greet them?" she suggested to Dagar.

He nodded and they mounted two horses and trotted out.

As they drew closer, she recognised the short, rotund man at the front. "It is the Bulgat tribe," she told Dagar and raised a hand in greeting.

Bat Khan raised his hand in response and Shuree's nerves settled. When he was close enough she said, "Welcome, Bat Khan. I am pleased to see you."

His eyes flicked to Dagar and then back to her. "Shuree. I hear you are the new khan. My condolences on the loss of your father."

The jolt of loss was one she was getting used to. "Thank you. Permit me to introduce Dagar, son of Ogodai Khan of the Erseg tribe."

Bat grunted. "I never thought I would see the day when we rode side by side."

"It is a new world," Dagar agreed. "One which we hope will prevail."

They entered the camp and Bat greeted those he knew. Shuree showed him where they could set up the tents they'd brought with them and invited them to her yurt for refreshments. Before they could settle, the Horkham tribe arrived and Turgen strode into her yurt, his orange tunic almost offensively bright.

"Don't mind me," he bellowed, pouring himself a drink.

Shuree smiled. "Turgen Khan, welcome to my yurt and my tribe." She introduced Dagar.

Turgen studied him and then turned to Shuree. "You'd better tell us why you think this ridiculous proposal of yours will work."

Shuree chuckled, not the least bit offended. Turgen was mostly bluster. She'd always enjoyed seeing him at their yearly summer gatherings. If she could convince these two men, they were well on their way to peace. "It will work, because we all want it."

A few days later the Kharil representatives rode into camp with Kublai Khan at the front, his thick, bushy beard resplendent.

Shuree invited the khans and spiritual advisors to dine with her along with Amar and Dagar. With members from five tribes, they represented half of Rhora.

"I want to thank you all again for coming," Shuree began. "It is heartening to see we are not the only ones who want peace."

Kublai held up his hand. "We have come, but we have not decided our stance yet," he said. "Peace is a lofty goal but so is trust." He glared at Dagar.

"Perhaps we can start by discussing what we each want," Dagar said. "That way we will have an idea of what we can offer each other."

Shuree nodded. "The Saltar tribe wish to live in peace, without fear from raid. We would like to trade with other tribes and learn from them. The Erseg horses are of fine stock and the Bulgat tribe have access to eagle feathers for arrows." She smiled. "I would also like more marriage between the tribes. When you grow up with the same people, it can be difficult to see them as a spouse."

Bat laughed. "I agree. My tribe is far healthier and happier since we began our yearly gatherings." He glanced at Shuree. "I was disappointed you turned down my son."

She flushed.

"Will others agree to trade when they can simply take it?" Turgen asked.

"I believe so," Dagar said. "I am not sure what the catalyst for the raids was. It must have been so long ago to have been forgotten from our memory."

Mengu spoke. "I have spoken with the other spiritual advisors and we all agree the Gods are ready for our fighting to end. As long as we control our tempers, we believe the khan gathering will strengthen this land and make the Gods happy."

They spoke into the night, debating and negotiating. As they finally left the yurt, exhaustion blanketed Shuree, but she was full of optimism. Amar hung back.

"I owe you an apology, Khan," he said. "You were right to hope, right to try something different. I haven't seen these men so animated in a long time."

She beamed at him, filled with relief. He had finally come around. "Thank you, brother. I would like your help in choosing the warriors to come with me," she said. "We must choose those who support our aims, but I am wary about leaving those who disagree behind without a strong leader to prevent them from spreading dissent."

He pursed his lips. "Gan is still making trouble, isn't he?"

She nodded. Though he hadn't been vocal in front of her, others had told stories of the lies he was spreading.

"I'll have another word with him."

"Thank you." She hugged him. Now he had given her support, she knew what to do. "I will leave you in charge when I go to the mountains. You will be able to temper disputes and ensure my wishes are carried out."

Amar smiled. "I'd be honoured." He left, disappearing into the darkness between the yurts.

"Do you truly trust him?"

Shuree jumped at Dagar's voice and turned to find him waiting beside her door. She placed a hand over her rapidly beating heart. "I do. Can I help you with something?"

"I have seen Amar speaking with Gan and it does not appear as if they are arguing. It surprised me he didn't defend your honour more when Gan insulted you."

"I can defend my own honour."

"And yet it is also a man's duty to defend those in his family." He stepped closer. "If I wasn't aware of how tenuous the trust is between our people, I would have beaten him until he had no more teeth."

In the light shining through her open door, his eyes were dark, anger simmering in them. A shiver went through her. He could be a very dangerous man. "I am not your family."

The intensity in his gaze took her breath away. "You are my hope… my people's hope for a better future."

She stepped closer, drawn to him. "Do you believe we can achieve what we want?"

He nodded and brushed a stray hair from her face. "There is something about you… I've not seen it before. Every khan in there let you lead the discussion, showed you utmost respect even though you are female and the first female khan any of the tribes has had in living memory. You inspire confidence and trust."

Pleasure and embarrassment swept through her and she glanced at her feet. "I was merely foolish enough to try something different."

Dagar lifted her chin. "I have spoken with the warriors who came with their khans. They all told the same story. The moment the women of their tribes heard what you had proposed, they all stood in support of you. In the Horkham tribe, the women stopped cooking and cleaning for the men, and wives wouldn't sleep with their husbands until they took your proposal seriously."

The feeling of his warm touch lingered on her chin. He was seducing her with his words.

No, she couldn't let it go to her head. Other tribes may not agree.

"Let's hope I can inspire the same in the remaining tribes." She stepped back, forced a smile. "I must get some sleep, so if there's nothing else you want?" She lifted her brows, waiting for his answer.

"Just one thing." He pulled her close and his warm lips covered hers.

Chapter 8

Shuree froze as her mind caught up to the fact that Dagar was kissing her. His lips were warm, gently brushing her mouth, and with a groan, she kissed him back. Hot, tingly sensations spread through her body. She'd been kissed before, but not like this. Not with so much intensity, Dagar's firm arms around her, him controlling every touch. She wanted more from him, but suddenly Gan's words sprang to her mind. She stepped back, pushed him away, catching her breath. "We can't do this."

"Why not?"

She shook her head, trying to clear it. She wanted to step forward again, into his arms. Instead she stepped back, into her yurt. The walls gave her strength. "There's too much at stake. I can't afford to be distracted."

He shifted, and smiled. "Isn't the point of the exercise to improve relations between our tribes?" he asked. "What better way to show you mean what you say?"

Shuree stiffened. "There are people in my tribe who already disagree with what we're attempting. If they see me kissing you, they'll think you've seduced me, think I'm not capable of leading, think I'm weak and easily led."

"There are those who already believe that," he said. "Why should we let them stop us? I admire you greatly."

He truly didn't understand how much more her actions would be judged because of her gender. "I can't risk it." She reached for the door. "Don't kiss me again."

The door closing shut off anything else he might have said. She exhaled and closed her eyes.

In any other situation she would follow her feelings, but she didn't dare now.

Out of everything she had done, everything she was attempting, why was this the most difficult?

***

"We should hold a wrestling tournament tomorrow," Turgen announced a few days after the Kharil tribe had arrived. "Our warriors are getting restless and it's best they are kept occupied."

"Good idea," Kublai responded. "Where's the best place, Shuree?"

"I'll get Amar to arrange it," she replied. Everyone enjoyed watching the tournaments which were held at the summer gatherings and it would be nice to have a day spent outside.

The next day, the sun shone brightly as most of the tribe gathered on the outskirts of camp. Shuree had let Amar choose the Saltar warriors who would take part and Gan was among them. Gan shouldn't be rewarded considering the unrest he was spreading, but perhaps Amar believed it would allow him to let off some steam.

Someone had erected pavilions for shade around where the wrestlers would fight. She joined the other khans and Dagar in the centre one from where they could see all the matches.

"Dagar, you should take part," Bat said, clapping Dagar on the shoulder. "You're the only Erseg warrior here, and my men need new challengers."

"Your men need to learn how to wrestle first," Kublai joked and all the khans laughed.

"That would leave us with an uneven number," Dagar said.

"You can sit out the first round," Turgen offered. "Then we'll draw names to see who will sit out during the next round."

Dagar glanced at the warriors, already shirtless and barefoot, spreading fat over their upper bodies to make them less easy to grip. "All right."

Turgen called out the pairs and then banged a drum for the fights to start.

Watching wrestling had never interested Shuree, but she cheered as Gan and then another of her tribe members made it through to the second round.

It was Dagar's turn to wrestle and he stripped off his tunic to reveal hard, rippled abs underneath. Suddenly the wrestling became far more interesting.

Over to one side, Tegusken and Badma viewed the wrestlers with interest, giggling and whispering to each other. Shuree hadn't had a chance to catch up with them in days. Badma pointed to Dagar and whispered something and then spotted Shuree. She waggled her eyebrows in Dagar's direction and grinned at her.

Shuree's cheeks flushed and she ignored her friends' laughter. Dagar was a warrior, so of course his body was strong.

The next round began and Shuree's attention was

fixed on Dagar, who wrestled one of Turgen's men. Turgen shouted encouragement as the men circled each other and then grappled. In a blink of an eye, Dagar flipped the Horkham warrior over his back and onto the ground. The man swore and Dagar gave him a hand up.

"Damn he's quick," Turgen murmured. Shuree didn't answer. She'd suspected Dagar would be a good warrior, though he had had the chance to study the fighters before his own match.

Dagar's opponent didn't seem too disgruntled as they moved into the crowd chatting. Gan glared after them, rubbing more fat onto his head in preparation for his next bout. He'd always bragged that shaving his head made him stronger, and gave his opponents less opportunity to grab him.

By the third round, they were down to three pairs and Turgen announced the matches.

"Dagar and Gan!" he called.

Shuree stopped listening. This was not a good match. Her concern was mirrored on Amar's face. She found Dagar in the line-up and his look of satisfaction added to her worry.

She turned to Turgen. "We should change the pairs," she said. "Gan hates Dagar."

Turgen laughed. "They're always the best matches." He patted her arm. "You'll see."

Before she could insist, he banged on the drum. Dagar and Gan circled each other as the crowd shouted. Neither seemed to notice the noise, their focus on their opponent, waiting for their move.

Finally Gan lunged forward, one hand finding Dagar's waistband and the other grasping his upper arm. They grappled, grunting, and moved in a circle, each trying to get the upper hand. Dagar twisted out of

Gan's grasp and came at him from a different direction, managing to lift him, but Gan shifted his weight and stopped himself from being thrown.

Shuree's heart thudded as they went at each other again, the slap of their skin making her wince.

Then, as before, Dagar shifted and Gan was thrown onto the ground—the match was over. Shuree sighed as Dagar held out a hand to help Gan up. Gan ignored it, reaching into his pocket and then lunged at Dagar. Something glistened in the sunlight.

"Knife!" Shuree yelled.

Dagar jumped back, narrowly being missed by the blade. Turgen roared, "Drop it!"

Gan ignored him and continued forward, slashing the knife towards Dagar. No one in the crowd moved.

Gan had gone too far this time. Shuree strode into the ring. "Gan, drop the knife immediately."

"You can't save your lover," Gan snarled. "He needs to die."

"Shuree, stay back," Dagar said.

She would not. She had to stop Gan from hurting Dagar.

"Stop it, Gan." Amar stepped forward out of the crowd.

"You're as weak as your sister," Gan spat. "Neither of you has any ability to lead."

Hurt and anger crossed Amar's face and he lunged at Gan's back, tackling him to the ground.

Gan roared in fury as Dagar joined the fray, blocking Shuree's view so she couldn't see what was happening.

Suddenly Amar yelled in pain and then a bloodied knife flew from the tangle of bodies.

Shuree flinched as Dagar pinned Gan, and Amar lay there, blood pouring from a wound in his stomach.

Fear froze her. She couldn't lose another brother.

Turgen strode forward to help Dagar restrain Gan and Shuree ran to Amar's side.

"I need a healer." She placed her hand over the wound and Amar groaned.

"Gan stabbed me." The disbelief in his tone was clear.

"Did it go deep?"

"I don't think so."

Hot relief swept over her. A healer joined them, looked at the wound and said, "Let's get him into a tent."

Shuree helped him to his feet. She wanted to go with her brother, make sure he was all right, but as khan she had to deal with Gan.

He was still struggling in Turgen's arms and icy cold fury filled her, every muscle in her body tightening ready for attack.

"Where do you want him, Shuree Khan?" Turgen asked.

Slowly she exhaled and forced herself to unclench her hands. "Take him to my tent." The anger in her words made Gan stop struggling, his mouth gaping a little. She would deal with him when she was calm.

Taking another breath, she bowed to Dagar. "My apologies, Dagar, son of Ogodai Khan. You were attacked in my home." Would he leave?

"This was not your fault," Dagar replied. "Go to your brother. We will talk afterwards."

The compassion and concern in his eyes helped diffuse the remaining anger.

The crowd around them were silent.

"The tournament is not over. Do you wish it to continue?" She directed the question at Kublai and Bat.

"We've had enough excitement," Kublai answered.

"Then let us prepare for dinner."

The crowd dispersed and Dagar followed the three khans and Gan back to her tent. Shuree went to find her brother.

He was lying on his back in the healers' tent while the healer stitched his wound and Nergui held his hand. When she walked in, he said, "I'm sorry, Shuree."

"You can't be blamed for Gan's actions." She took his other hand in hers and asked the healer, "How bad is it?"

"It wasn't deep, and didn't pierce any vital organs. He'll be fine."

Shuree exhaled, closing her eyes. "Good."

"What are you going to do to Gan?" Amar asked.

A good question. She wanted to kill him for hurting her brother, and for threatening the peace, but she'd always said violence wasn't the answer. "What do you think I should do with him?"

"Father would have beheaded him."

"Is that what you want me to do?"

He shook his head. "Gan's still grieving for his father."

"He can't go unpunished," Nergui said.

No, but if she banished him from the tribe, would it free him to cause more trouble?

The healer finished the stitches and cleaned the remaining blood from Amar's stomach. "No fighting until it heals," she said.

Amar sat up, wincing a little. Shuree hugged him. "Go show the tribe you are all right, and find out what people are saying. I must deal with Gan."

She headed for her tent. Gan's hands and feet were tied and he sat on the floor with Turgen, Bat, Kublai and Dagar standing over him.

"Thank you for your help." She poured them each a

drink and gestured for them to sit at the table. She stood over Gan. "What do you have to say for yourself?"

He spat. "I'm only sorry I didn't kill him."

She raised an eyebrow. "You wanted to kill your best friend?"

"Not Amar, the Erseg scum."

"You've broken the truce I made with Ogodai Khan and threatened our chance at peace. My father would have beheaded you for that."

His face paled, but he continued to stare defiantly at her. She wasn't ever going to change his mind. She turned to the other men in the room. "What would you do?"

"He refused to obey his khan's order as well," Bat pointed out. "It's more than enough to sentence him to death."

The other khans nodded.

"And what would you like me to do?" she asked Dagar. "It was your life he tried to take."

Dagar was silent for a long moment. "I trust your judgement to do what is right for your tribe."

The words burned through her leaving warmth in their trail.

She turned back to Gan and was reminded of his mother and how devastated she had been when her husband had died. Shuree couldn't take another life from her. She prayed to Qadan she wasn't making a mistake and spoke. "Gan, you are hereby banished from this tribe. You are no longer a member of the Saltar, you may not trade with us, stay with us or receive any help from us. You have thirty minutes to say goodbye to your family and gather your things."

Gan scowled. "I don't need this tribe."

Bat stepped up beside Shuree. "Gan, you are also

not welcome in the Bulgat tribe."

"Nor the Horkham tribe," Turgen said.

"If I catch you on Kharil lands, I will behead you," Kublai growled.

Gan's hands shook and his eyes were wide. Any friends he had in the other tribes were no longer available to him.

Dagar hauled Gan to his feet. "If you value your life, do not come near my tribe."

Half of Rhora was now forbidden to him. Shuree wasn't sorry. "Let's take him to his mother."

***

After seeing Gan's mother's tearful goodbye, Shuree wanted to close herself into her yurt and forget about the world. The woman's grief brought back Shuree's pain at losing her father and brothers, but Shuree was khan and she had to speak to her people about Gan's sentence.

She joined her brother by the communal fire and stood on the platform to get everyone's attention. "Today Gan drew a knife on our guest Dagar of the Erseg tribe and broke the truce we have in place with them. In the scuffle he stabbed my brother, Amar. As punishment he has been banished from the Saltar tribe."

A couple of people gasped. "The other khans were upset about this breach and have similarly banished him from their lands." Tegusken covered her mouth and others murmured. It might have been kinder to have simply killed him. "Gan was given time to gather his things and say goodbye to his family. He is no longer welcome on our lands and we will not trade or communicate with him."

Shuree swallowed. "If anyone else does anything to

threaten the peace we are trying to build, they and any co-conspirators will be beheaded. This is my only warning. You voted for peace and you each have a hand in making it a reality. If you hear of anyone unhappy with what we are trying to achieve, please speak to me." Enough people nodded to satisfy her. "Now, let's eat."

***

The messengers they had sent to the far west hadn't returned by the time they had to leave for the Dragon Mountains. Shuree prayed they were safe, that the other tribes had treated them well and not killed them on sight. She chose to take only Vachir and Erhi with her, rather than an extra four warriors as was her right. It was the best way she knew how to show she trusted the other tribes and was dedicated to the peace.

With her rode the seven members of the three eastern tribes as well as Dagar and Mengu. Spirits were high as the Saltar tribe waved them off.

They crossed out of Rhora on the third day and into the land known as Chungson. Erhi and the other spiritual advisors seemed to know where they were going as they led the party through the foothills. There were no roads, no paths, few signs of civilisation. Shuree had heard from traders that most Chungson people lived in the valley between the two main mountain ranges in the area, the Dragon Mountains and the Barrier Mountains.

They camped out in the open, the warriors taking turns to stand guard. As they travelled higher, Shuree regularly turned to look back the way they had come. The view over the expansive steppes was magnificent, her home laid out before her in all its glory. But at no stage did she see the other tribes making their way to the mountains. Shuree prayed to the Gods and ancestors they would come.

They entered the forest and its shade was cool and unfamiliar. The trees towered above and clustered around them. Shuree's muscles tightened. She was surrounded, unable to catch more than the occasional glimmer of blue sky. Perhaps the Gods were right to choose the Dragon Mountains as their gathering place. It was so foreign to them all, would leave them all discomfited and hopefully willing to negotiate quickly so they could return to their homes.

"Mengu says we should reach the meadow soon." Dagar's voice shocked Shuree out of her thoughts as he rode up beside her.

Her gut clenched. "I hope it is large and flat, with plenty of sky above us."

"Me too. These trees are confining."

She glanced at him and his smile was cautious. "You feel it too?"

He nodded.

"I'm glad I'm not the only one." They hadn't spoken about their kiss, and he'd made no further move to kiss her again, but it simmered unsaid between them. The more time she spent with him, the more she wished she was free to do what she wanted. "Will your father be there when we arrive?"

He glanced away. "I hope so."

Every nerve in her body stood on end. "What's wrong?"

He frowned. "Nothing."

Had she imagined the uncertainty in his tone? She checked no one was within earshot and lowered her voice. "Your father *is* coming?"

"The last update I received from him confirmed it." He lifted his head and scanned the tree tops.

Why was he avoiding looking at her? She wanted to

yank him around so she could see his eyes. "And he is bringing only five warriors with him." Maybe her unease at being in the forest was turning her paranoid. Dagar had never given her any indication he couldn't be trusted.

"That was the agreement." He nodded to Bat who rode ahead of them and had turned around.

Unable to resist, she grabbed Dagar's reins and pulled his horse to a halt, letting others move past them. "Will we be safe at the meadow?" Fear coursed through her veins. Were they walking into a trap? Ogodai hadn't set a time limit on the temporary truce. What if he'd only meant until they all arrived at the meadow?

"As far as I know." His eyes were full of confusion. "What's wrong?"

Vachir rode past. "Is everything all right?"

She forced a smile. "Yes, keep going. We'll bring up the rear."

Vachir didn't look convinced, but kept going.

When he was out of earshot she said, "There was uncertainty in your tone, Dagar." She stared into his eyes. "Am I being paranoid?"

He hesitated and then sighed. "No. I'm worried about those in my tribe who were vocal like Gan about not wanting a truce. My father says he made it clear to them that their opinions weren't wanted, but I keep thinking about Gan out there somewhere and worry he's making trouble." He turned to her. "I want this peace as much as you do."

Relief filled her. If that's all it was, they could deal with any mischief Gan caused. The khans had sent their tribes a message about Gan's punishment and it was unlikely the western tribes would trust him if they ran into him.

Up ahead a couple of people shouted and she nudged her horse faster to find out what was happening. They had arrived.

The meadow spread out in front of her, a flat plain of grasses and colourful flowers, with the beautiful blue sky above them. No one else was there. She sighed. Was that a good sign or a bad one? There were still two nights before the full moon. "Shall we set up camp in the middle?" she asked.

"Let's put the pavilion in the centre," Erhi said. "That way if the other tribes want to camp apart from us, they can."

She dismounted, leading her horse out of the shade of the trees, turning her face to the sky and the warmth of the sun. She was perhaps three horse lengths into the meadow when her horse whinnied and reared, almost pulling her arm from its socket. A roar echoed throughout the air and Shuree's heart leapt to her throat.

"Dragon!" someone cried.

Sure enough, three dragons, the size of small horses, swooped towards them, their leathery wings outspread and their focus on her. Magnificent and terrifying, glistening in the sun.

She fought to control her panicked horse but the reins ripped from her grasp and it bolted into the trees. The others were similarly fighting with their steads. The dragons opened their mouths and flames rushed towards the group.

Shuree dived to the side, feeling the heat from the fire, smelling the scorched grass.

Her pulse raced as she leapt back to her feet. Erhi had said the dragons lived further up the mountains.

"Shuree, get back under the trees," Dagar yelled.

Everyone else had taken cover.

The Gods had said to come here. They couldn't leave. The other tribes were expecting them to be there.

The dragons came around for a second pass. She knew little about the beasts. Some tales said they were intelligent creatures with their own society, but they might be as dumb as sheep for all she knew.

How dare you! The voice reverberated in her mind and Shuree fell to her knees, clutching her head. *We are nothing like sheep.*

Her mouth dropped open. Was the dragon speaking to her?

Well, it's not a sheep.

She almost laughed, but the dragons were nearing her again, in formation ready to attack. Dagar and Vachir ran out from the trees. Vachir gripped her arm to pull her up and Dagar aimed his bow and arrow at the dragons. Shuree lunged at him. "No, don't shoot them." She pushed them back under the trees as the flames chased their feet.

Her heart pounded. "Did anyone else hear them?"

"Hear who?" Vachir asked.

"The dragons. They spoke to me." She scanned the others until she found Erhi. "You said they live higher in the mountains."

Erhi shrugged. "I thought they did."

"What do you know about them?"

"Only that they are intelligent."

Then perhaps she could negotiate with them as well. "Everyone stay back, under the trees." She turned back to the meadow.

Dagar grabbed her. "You can't go back out there. They'll burn you alive."

She shook her arm free. "We need the meadow," she said. "I will talk with them."

The dragons circled the meadow, watching them.

Her body trembled as she stepped into the sunlight, not certain if she should speak aloud or with her thoughts.

Why are you here?

"Our Gods nominated this place as neutral ground for inter-tribal negotiations," she said, raising her voice so those behind her could hear. "It was not our intention to upset you. We did not realise you would be here."

She could feel the dragon's contempt. *Why do you think it's called Dragon Mountains?*

"I believed the dragons lived at the top." She turned on the spot, keeping the circling dragons in view. "My name is Shuree, khan… leader of the Saltar tribe. This gathering is very important to my people and I ask your permission to stay here in this meadow while we negotiate."

You, or all those people with you?

"All of us, and those still to arrive." She calculated quickly. "About forty more."

Tell me what is so important.

"Peace," she said. "We wish to stop the fighting between our tribes and be able to live harmoniously together on the steppes."

The dragon was silent for a long moment. *Your heart is pure, but I sense unease and uncertainty in your companions.*

"They are afraid of you and of what is to come. We do not know whether the others who are yet to arrive will keep the truce."

And yet you still came.

"Trust has to start sometime."

One dragon, a pale blue colour, flew low and landed lightly in front of her, tucking his leathery wings against his back. He was the size of a six-moon-old foal and his presence made her step back. He inclined his head. *I am Ghalin.*

Shuree bowed, her chest tight. "I am pleased to meet you, Ghalin."

Tell me exactly what you propose.

She explained the agreement she had negotiated with Ogodai, told him about her uncertainty about the tribes in the far west and let her emotions free as she spoke about what she wanted for her people. "All we want is to live in peace and stop the death of so many people."

Ghalin was silent a moment. *It is a noble cause.* He glanced behind her. *Please tell your companions you are safe. The one you call Dagar is very worried.*

She ignored the tug on her heart and waved to the group who were hovering at the edges of the trees. "I am fine," she called. "Ghalin and I are discussing what to do."

Ghalin snorted. *Some call you a witch for talking with me.* He puffed smoke from his nose and his amusement was clear. *I spoke with them. Now they wonder if they're going crazy.*

She chuckled, pleased the dragon had a sense of humour. "In truth, I do not know how long we will be here, and I cannot guarantee fighting will not occur. I can only promise you I will do my best to prevent violence."

Will you guarantee your people will not leave this meadow at all, or wander through the mountains?

"I can guarantee it for my people, but I will need to ask the other khans to guarantee for theirs."

Bring them out here so they can.

Shuree called them over and explained. Kublai, Bat and Turgen lined up and gave Ghalin their guarantees.

When do you expect the other tribes? Ghalin asked.

"Any day now," Shuree said.

We will watch for them and return for their promises. You

may stay for no more than one moon.

Relief filled her. "Thank you, Ghalin."

The dragon took flight and joined the other two who still circled, and together they flew off. She sighed, the tension in her shoulders releasing. She'd spoken with a dragon. Not something she'd ever imagined she would do.

She shook her head. The first challenge had been passed.

But there were many more to come.

Chapter 9

They set up camp on the far side of the meadow so the other tribes didn't feel nervous about approaching. In the centre, they erected a pavilion with open sides where discussions could take place. The first tribe to arrive a day later was the Gertan tribe which bordered Chungson. Seven mounted people hovered at the edges of the meadow and Shuree walked over to greet them, unarmed.

"I am Shuree, khan of the Saltar tribe," she said. "Thank you for coming."

The man in front with a long moustache touched the hilt of his sabre. "I am Oktai, khan of the Gertan. You brought more people than you said you would."

"No, I didn't." She smiled. "There are five tribes camped together. Please, join us."

"Dragon!" A warrior lifted his bow and arrow towards Ghalin above.

"No, don't." Shuree flung herself at the man, pulling his arm down. "Ghalin is friendly. We have an agreement with them. Let me explain."

The khan nodded, and the warrior lowered his bow.

"What agreement?"

We have permitted your tribes to stay in the meadow for your discussions, but no one may leave it for any reason while they are here.

The khan gasped, his eyes widening.

"That was my reaction too," Shuree said. "Ghalin has given us one moon to resolve our differences. You can choose to camp with us, or choose another location in the meadow if you like. The pavilion is where we will hold our meetings."

You have very little trust amongst each other, but we will not tolerate any fighting in the meadow.

"All right," Oktai said. "We shall camp nearby."

They rode past Shuree and chose a spot not too far away from the rest of the tribes. As she turned, Ghalin told her, *Another tribe will arrive within the hour.*

And so it went all day as the Danil, Marheg and Adhan tribes arrived. By nightfall, the only tribes not to arrive were the Erseg and Tungat. Tomorrow would be the full moon. Shuree found Dagar sitting by the campfire speaking with the Danil khan, Ulagan. "Excuse me, may I have a word with Dagar?"

The khan gestured for Dagar to go. Shuree walked with him away from the camp. Before she could speak, he said, "I don't know why they're not here yet."

Her skin prickled. "What is your relationship with the Tungat tribe?"

"It is close. My father's sister married their khan."

So they were family. And if the two tribes decided to ignore the agreement, they could easily wipe out the khans gathered here. She'd trusted Ogodai, had believed his word, but it was difficult not to worry. She kept coming back to Dagar's suggestion. Gan could have ridden straight to the Erseg and spread lies.

"Perhaps Ghalin can tell us where they are," Dagar said.

He might also be able to sense their intentions. "I'll see if I can contact him." Before she could walk away, Dagar grasped her hand.

"I am sure my father will not go back on his word." His thumb rubbed the back of her hand. "Surely you realise I wouldn't let anything happen to you. I care for you, Shuree."

She closed her eyes, glad of the darkness around them. "I told you I can't be distracted."

"What about afterwards?" he asked. "After this gathering, when peace has been achieved."

She paused. "Do you really believe peace is possible?" She heard the uncertainty in her voice. She had to stop showing her vulnerability to him.

"I do," he said. "We already have eight tribes willing to try. If Ghalin can find my father, and the Tungat, we will know for certain all will be here."

There was so much at stake. "All right."

He tugged her closer. "When this is over, I will return to our discussion about how I feel about you." He kissed the back of her hand and then rejoined Ulagan.

All the tribes sat around the large camp fire. Initially it had been the spiritual advisors who had approached each other, wanting to meet others like themselves. Then Turgen had spotted the Danils' superior wooden bows and asked about them, and soon they were intermingling, though each person was armed. Their level of defensiveness had lowered as they had all contributed to a communal meal. They were one people and it warmed Shuree even as she was troubled by Ogodai's tardiness.

She sighed and wandered further away from the fire. The twinkling lights danced in the sky above her, unhindered by any clouds. Would Ghalin hear her if she called him?

She closed her eyes and pushed the call out as far as she could. *Ghalin, can you hear me? I would like a word if you are near.*

A pause and then, *I don't need to be near to hear you.*

She smiled. *Do you know where the other two tribes are?*

Yes.

Shuree frowned. *Where are they?*

A long pause. *They will arrive early morning.*

Something in Ghalin's tone made her skin crawl. What wasn't he telling her? *Before sunrise?*

Another pause. *Yes.*

Her heart thumped. *Are they planning to attack?*

I am forbidden from telling you.

By whom?

My elders. We should not involve ourselves in human matters.

Shuree could feel he didn't agree with it. *Can you tell me how many people are with the two tribes?*

Twice the number that are gathered here.

She gasped, her stomach clenching. Ogodai hadn't honoured their agreement. What could she do? If she warned the others, they would be furious and would either leave, or want to attack first. But if she didn't warn them and Ogodai attacked, they would all be slaughtered.

Where are they camped?

About a league below.

Do they have any men watching the meadow?

Not any longer.

She couldn't scout them without at least telling someone where she was going. Her absence would be noticed. *Is there anything else you can tell me?*

Only that I disagree with my elders' orders.

This was going to end badly. She strode over to the

campfire, nerves prickling her skin. A couple of people looked up as she reached the firelight. "May I ask the khans to join me for a moment? Ghalin tells me the other tribes should arrive tomorrow and I would like to go over our agenda."

"Shouldn't we wait until they arrive?" Bat tapped absently on his round belly.

She forced a smile. "I think we can get much of the arguing done tonight."

A couple of people laughed, but the khans got to their feet. Vachir sat just in front of her and she tapped his shoulder and leaned close to speak. "Don't react, but don't let Dagar out of your sight. Get Erhi to watch Mengu."

He laughed as if she'd told a joke, but his eyes showed his concern.

She took a torch from the fire and led the khans over to the pavilion. When she turned, Dagar was there. Goat dung. She hadn't thought this through. He was his father's representative. She stared at him until Bat said, "What's this about, Shuree?"

"Ghalin gave me some disturbing news and we need to decide what to do about it."

"Do we need to leave the meadow?" Kublai asked.

"Maybe. I asked Ghalin when the other two tribes would arrive and he said early morning. When I questioned him further, he said they had twice our number of men and would arrive before dawn."

Dagar stepped back.

Kublai drew his sabre and pointed it at Dagar. "What is the meaning of this?"

Dagar didn't flinch. "I don't know. My father is not a trusting man, but I believed he would honour the agreement."

"We are supposed to have an arrangement with the

Erseg," the Adhan khan said. "But it appears he only really trusts the Tungat."

"Let me go and talk to him," Dagar said. "I can convince him you can all be trusted."

"No," Kublai said. "You will stay here as our hostage."

"We shouldn't stay at all. We're outnumbered," Ulagan said.

"I'll go," Shuree said. "He listened to me once before."

Bat laughed. "For all we know you're in on this too," he said. "I saw you speaking with Dagar in the dark."

"And you brought only one warrior with you," Kublai said. "Maybe it was because you knew Ogodai was bringing more."

Curse it. "We mustn't panic. Even if the Erseg and Tungat don't want peace, the rest of us do. We can still make a treaty."

"Not if we're all dead," the Marheg khan said.

"Ogodai may still only bring five warriors with him." Dagar turned to Shuree. "Where is he?"

She hesitated. "Ghalin said they're a league from here."

"That's a good distance if he leaves them behind."

"If," Bat stated.

Shuree could feel the trust slipping away. "Perhaps we can send scouts," she said. "When they break camp in the morning, the scouts can tell us how many men are coming and we'll have time to disperse if they bring all of them."

"If the scouts aren't caught."

Oktai twisted his moustache. "We need to calm down. Shuree is right. If we want peace, we must make it happen." Everyone turned to him. "In the dark, surrounded by forest, it shouldn't be difficult to disappear before Ogodai arrives if he brings too many warriors. Then we can meet at the base of the mountain to discuss a new plan."

Bat grunted. "I'll send a scout."

"So will I," Kublai said.

In the end, they all agreed to send a scout and that the Saltar and Erseg people would be guarded overnight. Shuree approved of the arrangement, if that was what they needed to trust her. The khans took them to a tent and posted a sentry inside and out.

Mengu and Erhi spoke quietly with each other while Vachir made himself comfortable on one of the beds, though he kept his gaze on Dagar.

"Shuree, I'm sorry—" Dagar said.

She held up a hand, her heart weary. "I am too tired for your apologies." She didn't know whether she could trust him anymore. Tomorrow would bring her answers. She lay down on the bedding, turning her back to him.

And prayed to the Gods like she had never prayed before.

***

Shuree slept poorly. After finally dropping off to sleep, every noise outside the tent woke her, from the squawk of a bird, to the steps of the guards outside and Mengu's heavy snores as he slept. Her eyes were gritty as she woke and the tent was a little lighter than the last time she'd opened her eyes. Was it almost morning? She sat up and the guard inside the tent looked over to her. Yes, definitely morning, she could make out the expression on his face. "Any news?" she asked quietly.

He shook his head.

Surely the scouts had made it back by now. Dagar

wiped his face with his hands. "Can we speak with the khans?"

"I'm under orders not to let you leave the tent," the guard said.

She closed her eyes. *Ghalin, any news?*

Silence.

Ghalin?

Still no response. Had he been punished for telling her as much as he had, or was he still asleep?

Outside were the sounds of people moving, a clank of a sabre, the rattle of a quiver. People were armed and preparing for battle. She glanced at Dagar and read the same concern on his face.

Suddenly the tent flap lifted and Kublai walked in. "Ogodai has arrived with the Tungat khan. They have nine warriors between them."

Relief filled Shuree and her body went limp. "May we greet him?"

Kublai nodded. "This way."

They joined the other khans who were lined up under the pavilion. Across the meadow stood a small group of a dozen people. The sun painted the ground in a dawn light and she picked Ogodai at the front, his posture erect. Next to him rode the man she assumed was the Tungat khan, and behind them were the rest of their men.

The group slowly made their way across the meadow, tension in their muscles, constantly scanning the surroundings as if expecting attack.

"May I go out to greet them, as I did with you?" she asked the other khans.

"Yes," Bat answered.

She stepped out from the pavilion and raised a hand in greeting, walking across the field towards them. When she was close, she called, "Greetings. I am pleased you could come. You are the last to arrive."

"Where is my son?" Ogodai asked.

"With the other khans under the pavilion," Shuree said. "When you have set up camp, we will meet there. You can choose to camp at any spot in the meadow, however the other khans have chosen to camp near us."

"They're really all here?" Ogodai asked.

She nodded. "They all want peace like we do."

He frowned. "Then how do you explain your scout?" He gestured and one of his men rode forward, pulling something behind him.

Gan stumbled into view, his face bruised and bloodied, defiance in every pore. "Shuree, the men are ready to attack when you give the signal."

Shuree gaped at him and then horror filled her at his words. "Gan is no scout of mine," she assured Ogodai, her pulse racing. "He was banished from my tribe for trying to kill Dagar."

Ogodai's expression darkened and he took the rope holding Gan from the warrior, jerking Gan towards him. "He said his name was Amar. He told me you've been forcing Dagar to write fake updates to make me lower my guard."

Gan smirked at her.

Shuree clenched her teeth. "Gan lies. Dagar can confirm it."

Ogodai glanced at the pavilion. "I want to see my son."

Shuree turned back to the pavilion and picked out Dagar next to Kublai. "He's the third man from the left." She waved the men forward and Dagar stepped into the dawn light.

Ogodai grunted. "I figured the scout was lying and now I know his name, it makes more sense. Dagar told me all about him." Ogodai drew his sabre and before Shuree could blink, he chopped off Gan's head.

Shuree gasped as blood flew into the air and Gan's body crumpled to the ground. She clenched her teeth to keep the bile at bay and stepped aside, a little dizzy, as Ogodai and his men rode past.

Justice was swift.

She took a moment to study Gan's body. He'd had his chances and wasted them all. She was only sad for his mother.

Moving back to the pavilion, she called to Ghalin. *The last two tribes have arrived, if you wish to get their agreements.*

No answer, however it was still early.

The two khans dismounted at the pavilion and handed their horses to their warriors, directing them to set up camp nearby. As Shuree caught up, Dagar was explaining who Gan was and making introductions. "Let's gather around the fire to eat," he suggested.

As they walked to the fire, Shuree pulled Kublai aside. "What happened last night?"

"The dragon lied. Ogodai didn't have any extra men with him. Our scouts checked the whole area but found nothing."

She frowned. "Why would he do that?"

A heavy flapping behind her made her turn as Ghalin came in to land. Shuree smiled, though was unable to keep her concern from her thoughts. "Good morning."

His posture was stiff. *You broke your promise, you must leave.*

The other khans turned back and Ogodai gasped. "Dragon."

Shuree shook her head. "What promise?"

You promised not to leave the meadow while you were here.

Her eyes widened. "But you said Ogodai had brought extra men. We needed to find out what he planned to do with them." Except he hadn't brought extra men. Her shoulders slumped. "You lied to me."

It was a test you all failed. You speak of trust and yet at the first sign, you did not.

She couldn't believe what he was saying. "I trusted you."

You know nothing of our kind. You trusted me over your own people.

Anger simmered. He was right, but it was only part of the story. "We could have left last night, disbanded because of your lies, but we didn't. We worked together to seek the truth."

You must leave.

"You manipulative creature," Kublai growled, unsheathing his sabre.

Violence is your first reaction to everything. Ghalin's disdain was clear as he glanced back to Gan's body. In the sky above, several dozen dragons flew in formation towards them. Shuree's heart raced.

She stepped forward. "No, it's not. Yes, we left the meadow, but we did not think of breaking our promise. We only went in the direction we had come."

"They're going to attack," someone yelled behind her. "Get your weapons!"

Peace was unravelling before her. Ghalin flapped his wings ready to take flight, and next to her, Kublai shifted to attack. She couldn't let this happen.

"No!" She leapt in front of Ghalin as Kublai thrust his sword. The sharp blade pierced her stomach, slicing with red hot pain. She gagged, clutching the blade as absolute horror crossed Kublai's face and he let go of the hilt. Sweat prickled her skin and it was impossible to breathe.

"Shuree!" Dagar yelled.

She stumbled back, almost crashing into the dragon. Her knees buckled and she fell to the ground, tears streaming down her face. The sabre shifted, widening the wound. The morning dew soaked her pants adding some coolness to the fire shooting through her arms, stomach, legs.

Around her people yelled, but nothing made sense. All she knew was she couldn't let them kill the dragons. Gasping, she whispered, "Don't fight." She swallowed and raised her voice as loud as she could. "Don't fight each other, don't fight the dragons."

Why did you do that? Ghalin asked, his confusion clear. *I can protect myself.*

"Too. Much. Death."

Dagar dropped to his knees beside her, devastation on his face. "Shuree."

She blinked at him, her brain working slower now. Warm blood flowed over her hands and together Kublai and Dagar helped her to lay down. She was dying. She'd seen similar injuries before and knew there was no recovery. Still she couldn't see all that she'd worked so hard for be ruined. She gripped Dagar's hand. "Peace." Every word was torture.

"Hold on, Shuree." He looked around and yelled, "Don't we have a healer?"

She doubted any of the khans had used one of their precious warrior places on a healer.

"You can't die, Shuree. I won't let you." The fierce determination on his face made her ache.

"I'll find you on the endless steppes," she whispered, her eyes fluttering closed.

"No!"

I can help, Ghalin said. *We have a healer.*

"Haven't you done enough?" Dagar growled.

Shuree forced her eyes open. "Trust."

A green dragon entered her field of vision. *This will hurt,* the female voice said. *Take out the sabre.*

Dagar and Kublai both hesitated. She was dying anyway. "Trust," she repeated.

Dagar nodded and Kublai withdrew the blade. Sharp, slicing pain. Darkness claimed her.

Chapter 10

Silence surrounded Shuree. Her body was heavy, her mind thick and she struggled to make sense of where she was, and what was happening. She tried opening her eyes, but even her lids were as heavy as a new-born foal.

"Shuree?" Dagar squeezed her hand.

Why was he holding it? What would the others think?

Shuree, open your eyes. You need to drink. The gentle feminine voice in her mind was insistent.

She tried again and this time light seeped through the gap in her eyelids, forcing her to blink.

"You're alive." The relief in Dagar's voice was evident.

Why wouldn't she be alive? What was going on? She turned her head and found she was in a tent and a green dragon was by her bed. "What—" Her lips cracked and her voice broke. It was too difficult to speak.

Dagar helped her to sit and held a cup of water to her mouth for her to sip. "You got in the way of Kublai's sword."

You saved Ghalin.

Memories flashed back to her and she touched her stomach. No pain, no injury at all. "I was dying."

The anguish on Dagar's face was heartbreaking. "Lelin saved you." He indicated the green dragon with icy blue eyes, who was smaller than Ghalin.

"How?"

I can heal your tissue, knit it back together, but you have lost a lot of blood. You will be weak for a few days.

There was so much they didn't know about the dragons. "Thank you." She lifted her tunic, but the skin on her stomach was smooth, unmarked. Incredible.

Thank you for saving Ghalin. After what he did, we are surprised you acted that way.

"I didn't want him hurt." Her head spun as she shifted away from Dagar. "Where are the others?"

"They're meeting together," Dagar said.

"Without me?" She stood and stumbled, falling into Dagar's arms.

"Easy," he said, one firm arm around her, supporting her weight. "When they realised you would survive, they started the discussions. They thought it would be nice if they could get most of the arguing done before you arrived, show you they could negotiate without you there."

She let him lower her to the bed. "They're not trying to keep me out because I'm a woman?"

"After what you've achieved, they wouldn't dare," Dagar said. "You've impressed them all. Kublai feels particularly indebted to you."

She would have to talk to him later. "I'd like to go out."

"You should rest."

"I can rest under the pavilion as easily as I can rest here," she said. "And there might be food out there."

He scowled and looked at Lelin.

She will be fine.

Dagar wasn't pleased. "I will take you, but you're not walking. I'll carry you."

She shook her head. "That will make me seem weak."

"Didn't you say people thought you talking to my tribe was weak, and yet you did it anyway, and here we are."

He was right. "All right." As long as she was part of the discussions, it didn't matter how she got there.

He lifted her easily and carried her out of the tent. It was close to midday and warriors were spread through the camp. Someone had set up targets across the meadow and it appeared an archery tournament was underway. Nearby one of the Horkham warriors was wrestling with an Adhan man and others stood around cheering them on. Over by the horses, an Erseg man stood proudly beside his horse, chatting to two other men who were admiring the beasts. It was a community, much like any tribe.

"Where's Gan?" she asked.

"We buried him," Dagar replied.

She would have to tell his mother and Amar when she returned. Dagar carried her to the pavilion and set her down next to Erhi and Vachir.

"Shuree, we are glad to see you up," Kublai said.

"We weren't sure how long you'd be, so we started," Ogodai said.

She smiled. "I am glad. I didn't hear any arguing from the tent, so does that mean you've moved past that stage?"

The men laughed. "We have," Bat said. "Let me fill you in."

Someone tapped her on the shoulder and Dagar

handed her a bowl of soup. "Thank you."

She sipped the meaty broth as the khans each told her the items they were willing to trade and how they had agreed with her idea of an annual gathering to foster communication and understanding between the tribes.

"They ask we split our harvest with them," Vachir said, "And I thought we could maybe increase the land we sow."

An interesting idea. Some people preferred staying in one place. "We can definitely investigate it." The broth helped her energy but it was still difficult to hold herself upright. Her limbs were weak and her head a little light. Perhaps she'd been too quick to come out here. She swayed a little and Dagar sat next to her.

"Lean against me," he murmured.

She was too tired to care what anyone thought. Dagar's body was a warm, solid wall and she liked the feel of his arm around her. The khans discussed options, argued about details and she added her opinion when it was needed. By the time it grew dark and Erhi called an end of the day's discussion, Shuree was having difficulty keeping her eyes open.

"Have something more to eat, and then go to sleep," Vachir said. "I'll keep an eye on things here." He gestured to the khans.

"I don't think you have to," she said. "They seem to be getting along just fine."

"Thanks to you," Dagar whispered.

His breath tickled the back of her neck. He helped her to her feet and swept her into his arms again. She didn't protest. She was too tired to walk.

As they made their way back to her tent, Kublai joined them. "I am so sorry, Shuree."

She placed a hand on his arm. "It was an accident. I

don't blame you."

"I'm relieved the dragon could save you."

"What happened to Ghalin?"

"He flew away with the other dragons after Lelin healed you," Dagar said.

She would like to speak with him again before they left.

"Speak of the devil." Kublai pointed to where both Ghalin and Lelin were coming in to land, the power in their muscles and their massive wing span still awe-inspiring.

"Put me down, Dagar." She shifted and he set her on her feet, keeping an arm around her waist. Nerves tickled her belly.

We have come to see how you are, Lelin said.

And to apologise. Ghalin lowered his head.

"Then please, come to my tent," Shuree invited.

Before she could ask, Dagar picked her up again. She could get used to being carried by him.

Inside her tent, he placed her on the bed and the dragons entered, Ghalin slinking in looking distinctly uncomfortable at the walls surrounding them.

Lelin approached Shuree. *May I touch you to see how you are healing?*

"Yes."

Lelin placed her paw on Shuree's arm and a soft, probing sensation filled her body. *Still some ways to go. Dagar, could you get her more food?*

"Can he be trusted?" Dagar glanced at Ghalin.

I was under orders. I am sorry. Ghalin sounded genuinely bereaved.

But he'd admonished her for trusting him over her own people... She sighed. Trust had to start somewhere. "I'll be fine. I am hungry and thirsty."

Dagar studied her and then turned to Ghalin. "If

you harm her, you won't leave this camp alive." He walked out.

Ghalin moved a little closer but stopped about a yard from the bed. *I did not want to lie to you, but my elders asked it of me. Interactions with humans are rare and it was us who didn't trust.*

She frowned. "Why try to sabotage our attempts at peace?"

If you are busy fighting each other, you have no time to come into our mountains. We have seen how quickly humans can spread.

"You were trying to protect your home." It was something she could understand.

The elders send their apologies. They thank you for saving me.

"And I thank Lelin for healing me." She pursed her lips. "If I could ask one thing of you?"

Go ahead, Ghalin said.

"I ask that your kind do not lie to us in future. You have the advantage of hearing our thoughts, and knowing if we lie, but we do not have the same advantage. I would like to be able to trust you going forward."

Ghalin was silent and Lelin said, *He is asking the elders.*

Finally Ghalin spoke. *The elders agree. We will not lie to humans again.*

"Thank you."

Lelin shifted. *As payment for our actions, we have given you a gift.*

Shuree frowned. "That is not necessary. Your promise not to lie is enough."

It is necessary. Your goal here was pure and we corrupted it, Ghalin said.

She could feel his insistence. "Very well. What is the

gift?"

It is nothing you can see, Lelin said. *It is inside you.*

She pressed a hand against her stomach, unease making it swirl. "I don't understand." What had they put inside her when she was unconscious?

It will be passed on to your children, and if they are worthy, it will be passed onto theirs through the female line.

What were they talking about?

Your strength has always been compassion, Ghalin said. *This will be enhanced so when you leave this place you will spread it through the tribes, and achieve the peace you hope to attain.*

Lelin nodded. *Your children may have need of a different gift—that of healing, or helping plants grow,* she explained. *When they reach the age of eleven, you will need to decide what their gifts should be.*

They spoke of magic. "And if they don't want it?" Shuree asked.

Ghalin answered. *They can choose not to use it at all.*

We will watch you, Lelin said. *When the time comes, you can come to us for help or answers.*

It was hard to comprehend, but if no harm would come to her or her children, she would accept it. "Thank you." Later, when she wasn't so tired, and peace had been negotiated, she would ask for more details.

We have one more thing to ask of you, Ghalin said. *We would like to listen to your discussions, learn about you.*

"I am happy for you to, but the other khans must agree."

Dagar returned with a bowl of dumpling soup. "Is everything all right?"

"It is." She took the soup from him. "Ghalin would like to sit in on our discussions tomorrow. Could you ask the khans whether they agree to it?"

He raised an eyebrow. "Is that wise?"

"A lack of understanding brought us here. Let's not repeat the same mistakes as we made with our own people."

He shook his head. "You are too lovely to be real." He caressed her cheek and walked out.

Her heart beat a little faster. When this was over, she would have to do something about her feelings for Dagar.

He would make a strong father for your children, Lelin said.

Shuree gaped at her.

Something to think about. Lelin exposed her teeth in a smile.

Shuree didn't reply, though Lelin could probably see her thoughts.

Peace had to be achieved first.

***

It took another five days to negotiate the terms of the peace treaty. Arguments broke out regularly after the first day; perhaps with Shuree's health improving, the men no longer felt like they needed to hold back their emotions. A few times they had to break up the meeting to give people time to cool off and each time Shuree went to speak with those involved to help them see the situation from the other's point of view. On one such time she wandered over to where Turgen was shooting arrows at the targets, his movements fast and his whole body tense.

"Are you pretending it's Ogodai you're shooting?" Shuree asked as she stood next to him.

Turgen swore. "That imbecile!"

Shuree waited until he'd used all the arrows in his quiver and then walked over to the target with him to withdraw them. "I can't say I agree with his phrasing," she said. "Our women should not be traded, and there should be no minimum number who move tribes, but arranging suitable love matches between the tribes would be good for everyone."

"He wants my daughter for his wife. He's older than I am!"

"Then perhaps we need to add a clause that no one may be forced into a marriage they do not want. Then your daughter can choose whether she wants to marry Ogodai."

"She won't want to."

"Then you have nothing to worry about." She slid the arrows into his quiver.

The simmering tension in him deflated and he rubbed the back of his neck, sighing. "You're right. My anger made me lose focus."

She smiled. "It's been a long few days. Why don't you shoot another quiver of arrows and I'll chat to Ogodai? Then we can arrange for more food and continue the discussions."

"All right."

As she approached Ogodai in his camp, the khan held up his hand. "Don't speak. Dagar has already explained how my words were misconstrued and I know your feelings about women being commodities."

"Glad I can save my breath." She grinned at Dagar. "Turgen has calmed down. We're going to get some more food and reconvene shortly."

He waved her off. "I'll be there."

On her way to her tent, Kublai stopped her. "Shuree Khan, I wish to discuss something of a personal nature with you."

Surprised, Shuree nodded. "I was heading for my tent. Why don't you join me?"

Kublai waited until they entered before he said,

"This talk of intertribal marriages made me think." He accepted the drink she handed him. "You are not married and I have a son who is unmarried."

She raised her eyebrows at him and he grinned, stroking his beard. "My son would be lucky to have such a strong and compassionate wife such as you."

Shuree knew the son Kublai was discussing and he had only ever been a friend to her. "You honour me, Kublai Khan, however I do not wish to marry your son."

Kublai sighed as if expecting her answer. "It couldn't hurt to try. I suspect I was too slow in my offer. Someone else has captured your attention."

Her cheeks warmed. "My only concern right now is finalising this treaty."

"Just make sure you do not wait too long and lose the opportunity." He gulped his drink and slammed the cup on the table. "I'm sure Turgen's had enough time to cool down. Let's get back to it."

Shuree picked up the food she'd come for, and followed him out of the tent.

On the final day, after the spiritual advisors had retired to write the final document, Kublai stood. "I want to propose one last thing."

A couple of men groaned and Ogodai called, "We've already agreed to everything."

Kublai shook his head. "If there is a disagreement between the tribes, we need someone who can resolve it—an arbiter—so that we don't resort to violence," he said. "It will be too difficult to call all the khans together quickly to make a decision, so we need one person we can go to—a Great Khan."

"Won't it mean the person has more power than the rest of us?" Ogodai asked.

"To a degree," Kublai said. "They'll resolve disputes between the tribes and can be responsible for ensuring the treaty is maintained."

Shuree shifted. It was a large responsibility to put on one person.

"How do we choose them?" Bat asked.

"I'll nominate myself," Ogodai said.

Kublai shook his head. "All the khans must vote for the Great Khan. We can do it at the annual gathering and the person must have all the tribes' support. That way we do not get stuck with someone who has their own agenda." He raised his eyebrows at Ogodai and then said to the others, "What do you think?"

"It's a good idea," Shuree answered. "Should the person be a khan, or should we choose one of our tribe members for the role?"

"Whoever is suitable," Bat said. "Though I would hope at least one of us would be."

A couple of people laughed.

"Raise your hand if you are in agreement," Kublai said.

Shuree raised her hand along with the others.

"Then we must choose a Great Khan," Kublai said. "I nominate Shuree Khan of the Saltar tribe."

Shock speared Shuree and she stared at him, her mouth open. The men before her had far more experience than she did. She tried to protest but no words came out.

"I second it," Bat said. "We wouldn't be here without her."

Ogodai glared at her and then smiled, suddenly looking so much like Dagar that Shuree blinked. "I agree. Shuree would make the perfect Great Khan."

Her chest expanded but she couldn't breathe. Tears welled in her eyes as one by one the other khans chimed in with their agreement. This was the last thing she'd ever imagined when she'd started this. She couldn't believe they had so much faith in her. Could she actually do this?

It is exactly because you don't want this, that you are perfect for the role, Ghalin said.

Maybe he was right. She exhaled and clenched her hands together to stop them from shaking.

"Do you accept the nomination, Shuree?" Kublai asked.

Each khan watched her with faith in their eyes. She swallowed and nodded. "I accept."

"Then I announce Shuree as the first Great Khan of Rhora," Kublai said.

The men all raised their glasses and toasted her.

The light-headed feeling had nothing to do with the blood she'd lost days earlier. "Thank you."

***

While the khans went to gather by the campfire for dinner, Shuree wandered in the opposite direction. She needed fresh air and solitude to absorb what had just happened. Not only was she khan for the Saltar tribe, but for the whole of Rhora as well. The responsibility weighed on her and her steps felt heavy, as if she'd had too much litak to drink.

What would her father think of all that had happened? She could almost hear Yul's voice in her head encouraging her. Her eyes watered.

Why are you surprised? Ghalin asked, trotting up next to her.

She blinked away her tears. "I didn't ask for this. I only wanted peace."

And you have it now. Your people recognise they would not be here if it weren't for your strength. My elders wouldn't have agreed to giving you the gift if they hadn't seen the goodness in your heart.

"Is that why they voted for me?" Shuree asked. "Because of the gift you gave me?"

He shook his head. *Kublai had the idea long before we gave you the gift.*

It had to be useful being able to hear someone's thoughts.

Sometimes. He glanced over his shoulder. *I will leave you now and return tomorrow to say goodbye.* He took to the sky. No matter how many times she saw it, the image filled her with such awe.

"Shuree."

At Dagar's call, she turned. She hadn't seen him much over the past few days. He hadn't attended the meetings and she had been too tired in the evenings to do more than eat and go to bed. He stopped a few feet away from her and rubbed the back of his neck, his movements a little stiff. She smiled. "Dagar. How are you?"

"Relieved you have recovered well." He studied her as if looking for signs of strain.

"I have," she said. "Though Kublai nearly shocked me to death when he put my name forward as the Great Khan."

"I heard. Congratulations."

She clasped her hands together. "Thank you, though I don't believe I deserve it."

"Why not?"

"I know little about being a khan."

He smiled. "And yet you brought peace to us all." He stepped closer and took her hands to stop her fidgeting. "You need to have as much faith in yourself as I have in you."

She owed him an apology. "I'm sorry for not

trusting your father."

He sobered. "Even I doubted him when Ghalin lied to us, so you have no cause to apologise."

She turned her hand and clasped his. All that was left was to sign the treaty. Could she now follow her own desires, take something she wanted for herself? Then she remembered something he'd said when she'd first met him. "Why didn't you want to be khan?"

He frowned at the change in topic. "I never wanted to be the one to order warriors into battle. Like you, I saw the grief it caused."

She cupped his cheek. "That's very noble."

"Perhaps now it is considered so." He held her hand in place and leaned into it. "Shuree, we leave tomorrow. I don't want to go without telling you how I feel."

Her heart skipped a beat and she waited for him to continue.

"You captured my attention the moment you spared my brother and have been in my thoughts ever since. The more I've grown to know you, the more my admiration for you has increased. You are the strongest woman I have ever known."

The intensity of his gaze made it impossible to look away.

"When you were stabbed I realised how much I've come to love you, and the idea of leaving you breaks my heart."

She couldn't resist his vulnerability. She kissed his lips, softly, briefly, absolutely certain about what she wanted. "You treated me like your equal from the moment we met. Your respect for me gave me strength and hope." She smiled at him. "I hate the idea of the man I love leaving." She had already broken so many conventions being a warrior and a khan. Now she would break one more. She inhaled deeply, wanting to remember this moment. "I find myself in need of a Tribal Father, a husband, and a partner. Would you consider the role?"

His jaw dropped and then he grinned. "I would. I will. Yes." He picked her up and swung her around and then kissed her deeply. She clung to him, giddy. When he set her down, he held her close and then he chuckled.

"What's so funny?"

"You do realise, you'll have to negotiate our betrothal with my father?"

She groaned and glanced over his shoulder at the camp. Ogodai watched them, eyebrows raised. How much of her harvest would she have to surrender? She smiled. It didn't matter. "You're worth it."

Epilogue

The next morning, after signing the treaty and saying goodbye to Ghalin and Lelin, the tribes journeyed down the mountain together. When they reached the foothills, the western tribes split off to head home. Shuree promised them she would see them soon. The khans had agreed she needed to tour the ten tribes before the first summer gathering to lessen their people's fear of change. And knowing what Lelin had said about her compassion spreading to the other tribes and enhancing peace, she had agreed.

She had told no one about what the dragons had given her, too uncertain about how it worked to put it into words. Besides, the risk was too great that it might scare someone and the peace would falter. Eventually, when she understood it better, she would tell the others, and hopefully by then Rhora would have been at peace for many years.

The other tribes accompanied her home.

As they rode closer, she noticed people rushing about, many of them mounting horses, ready to form a defence. She raised her hand. "Let me go on ahead. They look a little concerned." She kicked her horse into a gallop and waved when she recognised Jambal standing guard.

"It's Shuree!" he yelled and Amar rode out to greet her.

"Sister, you ride with more company than you did before."

"They are friends, all of them." She waved them to approach and scanned the warriors around her. This could be the last time they scrambled to defend the tribe. She smiled, pleased to be home. "Let us arrange a communal dinner so I can tell you everything that has happened."

"Are you sure they're friends?" He eyed Dagar as he rode up.

"I am. You've met my betrothed, Dagar." She and Ogodai had haggled the groom price on the way down the mountain.

Amar's mouth dropped open. "Your betrothed?"

"Yes."

"But I did not approve it."

"I am khan," Shuree reminded him. "I do not need your approval."

He scowled as they rode into the camp and Shuree showed the other tribes where they could set up their tents. Badma ran to her. "You're back! How did it go?" She flung her arms around Shuree, and Shuree hugged her back.

"It went better than I could have imagined," she whispered. "We are at peace. Gather everyone around the communal fire. We have a story to tell."

Nergui was slower in her approach, but no less enthusiastic. "My grandchild, the Gods have answered my prayers to see you safely home."

She squeezed her grandmother. "They have been listening to us both," she said. "Permit me to introduce my betrothed, Dagar."

Nergui hugged him. "Welcome back, Dagar of the Erseg tribe."

Others did not appear as pleased, but they would learn soon enough that times had changed.

As the sun set, Shuree stood on the same stage where her tribe had made her khan. With her were the other khans, Ogodai standing side-by-side with Bat, his tall leanness in direct contrast with the rotund man, and Bat and Kublai were next to the Adhan and Tungat khans.

She introduced them and then announced, "The ten tribes of Rhora have signed a peace treaty. No longer will we fight amongst ourselves, killing and stealing. From now on, we will trade and help each other." She explained the terms of the treaty and then Kublai stepped forward.

"We agreed there must be someone the tribes can go to if there are disputes, to prevent us falling back into old ways. We decided we must have a Great Khan, one person who can arbitrate disagreements." He gestured to Shuree. "All of the khans agreed Shuree shall be our Great Khan."

She blushed, still not used to the title as the reactions went from shock to pleasure, and then her tribe broke out in cheers. She swallowed hard and held up a hand for silence. "I am honoured by the title. It will be awarded each year at the summer gathering, but this year I shall travel from tribe to tribe so they may get to know me and not fear this change. I will take with me my betrothed, Dagar of the Erseg tribe, a man I chose, who is not part of the treaty agreement." She wanted that clear. "In my stead I leave my brother in charge as he has led you over the past moon." She took a breath. "It is now time to eat, but I hope you will make the khans, spiritual advisors and warriors feel welcome."

She stepped down, pulling Dagar with her.

"I saw some unhappy faces," he murmured, keeping his hand in hers.

But they were in the minority. "There will be a few. We shall stay here for a little longer so I can ensure there is no confusion about my orders and then we shall start our journey to the other tribes."

"I shall look forward to spending more time in my new home."

She turned to him then. "Do you mind moving?"

He shook his head, pulling her close. "I will see my tribe every summer and they are close enough for me to visit, should I wish to. It is you I cannot imagine living without."

Her heart swelled. "We shall make our home together in the new Rhora."

And they would prosper with the newfound peace.

Thank you for reading!

I hope you enjoyed visiting Rhora. If you want to discover how the Rhoran fare in the future, make sure you read the rest of The Emperor's Conspiracy series, starting with The Assassin's Gift.

Acknowledgements

This story wouldn't exist if not for Lana Pecherczyk and Michelle Diener. They thought up the idea behind the Fantasy Realms Warlord, Witches and Wolves anthology and I needed to come up with a story for it. It didn't take too long to realise telling the story of the Great Khan would be a perfect match.

I want to also acknowledge Shuree Tumursukh who helped me with all of the Rhora name pronunciations for The Assassin's Gift audiobook. Shuree Khan is named for her.

The Assassin's Gift

The Emperor's Conspiracy #1

She's trained to kill. But is her prey the man she's ordered to eliminate… or the one who sent her?

Princess Lien reserves her loyalty for her uncle, the emperor. Groomed as his secret assassin after he took her in, her first target is the khan of the barbarians responsible for her parents' murder. But her supernatural speed is no help when the monarch betroths her to the man she's meant to slay.

Waking naked in the enemy camp far from the palace and her pet dragon, Lien is horrified to find she's imprisoned by the ruthless tribe—and they know her true mission. Refusing to believe her uncle betrayed her, she vows to become his spy. But as evidence that she's on the wrong side mounts, it will test her fidelity and honor.

Can Lien unravel a web of deceit in time to stop the real traitor?

The Assassin's Gift is the first book in the riveting Emperor's Conspiracy fantasy series. If you like strong heroines, loyalties challenged, and treacherous battles, then you'll love Claire Leggett's enthralling adventure.

Buy *The Assassin's Gift* to reveal the heart of evil today!